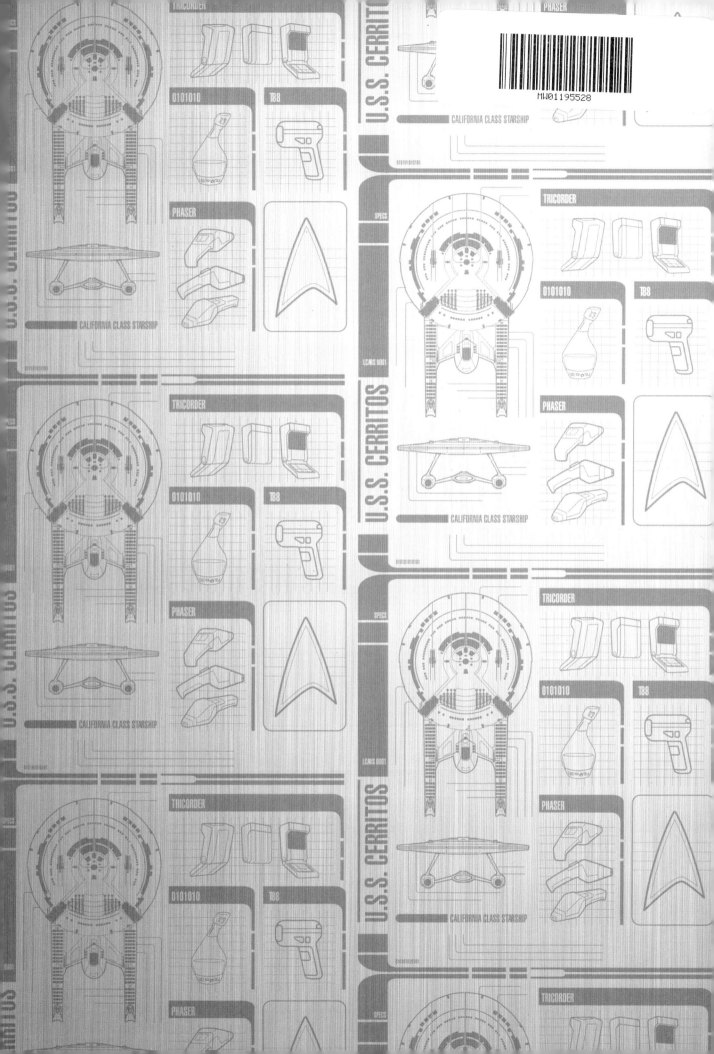

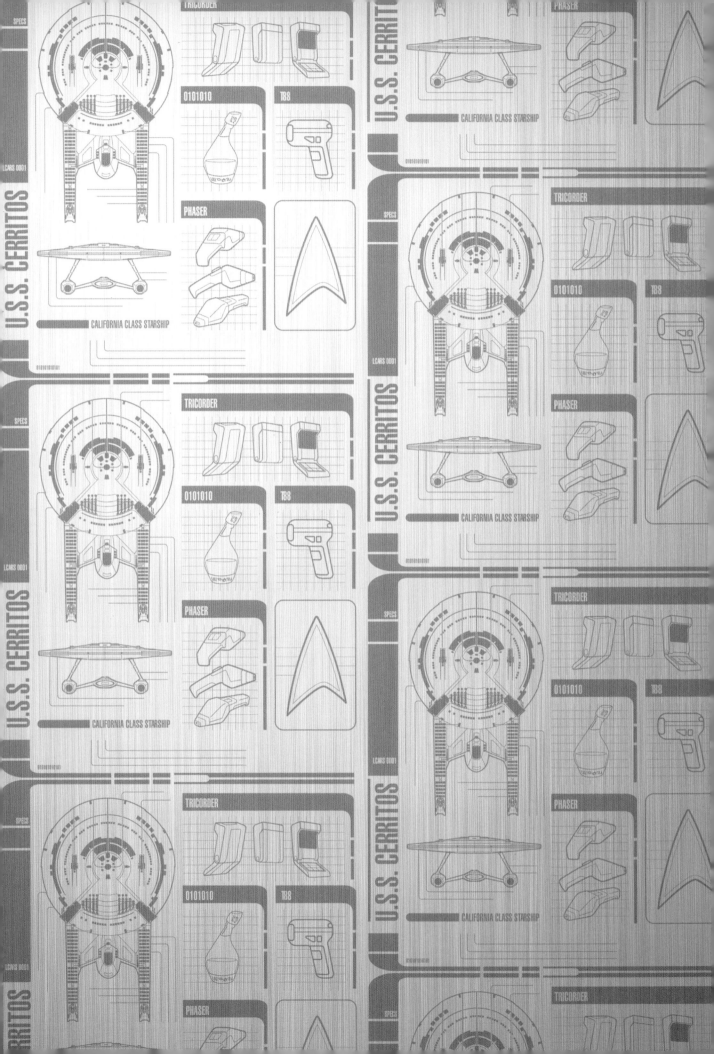

STAR TREK™
LOWER DECKS
U.S.S. CERRITOS
CREW HANDBOOK

Published by Titan Books
A division of Titan Publishing Group Ltd.
144 Southwark St.
London
SE1 0UP

First edition: October 2023
2 4 6 8 10 9 7 5 3

startrek.com

Did you enjoy this book? We love to hear from our readers.
Please e-mail us at: readerfeedback@titanemail.com
or write to Reader Feedback at the above address.

To receive advance information, news, competitions,
and exclusive offers online, please sign up for
the Titan newsletter on our
website: www.titanbooks.com

A CIP catalogue record for this title is available from the British Library.

STAR TREK
Lower DECKS
U.S.S. CERRITOS
CREW HANDBOOK

CHRIS FARNELL

TITAN BOOKS

CONTENTS

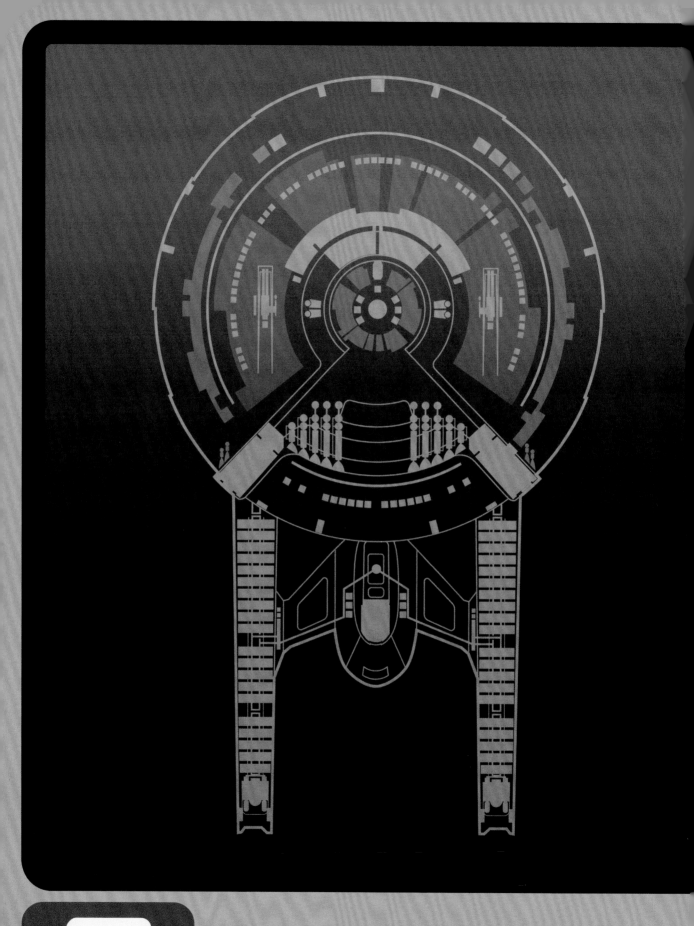

U.S.S. CERRITOS
CREW HANDBOOK

FREEMAN:

Lieutenant Junior Grade Boimler, please ensure the replicators are programmed using the draft USS_Cerritos_crew_handbook_complete_Final_draft_v4.5_FINISHED_Usethis_2_CLEAN. I'm sure you can imagine how embarrassing it would be if we replicated several hundred copies of this book covered in corrections and editorial feedback!

MESSAGE FROM THE CAPTAIN:

If you are reading this then you have been newly transferred to the *U.S.S. Cerritos* NCC-75567. To come this far you must have excelled in your chosen field, surpassing exemplary standards of academic achievement, technical skill, tactical ingenuity, and physical fitness, and that is before you underwent the demanding rigors of the Starfleet Academy training program.

You have done well to get this far. You will find the *Cerritos* is a fine ship. We may not get the big, splashy, glamorous jobs like the *Enterprise*, or the thrill-a-minute, derring-do adventures of the *Titan*, or the bleeding edge technology of the *Dauntless*, but we get the job done and, hey, at least we're not an *Oberth* class!

We on the *Cerritos*, alongside our *California*-class sister ships, perform a vital function to the planets of the Federation and beyond. Through our twin roles of second contact and engineering support, we go where Starfleet ships have gone before to follow up on their work and, occasionally, clean up their mess.

But we can only carry out this mission if everyone plays their part. As a junior officer aboard the *Cerritos*, we rely on you to uphold Starfleet's values, obey orders, and, above all, follow procedure to the letter.

This is why we are issuing you our new edition of the *U.S.S. Cerritos Crew Handbook*. The old edition was getting… a little outdated so we relish the opportunity to create a new handbook with everything our crew members need to know, compiled for the junior officers, by the only junior officer to volunteer for the job.

What's more, at great expense (a figure of speech, obviously, as we don't use money and everything is free) this handbook has been issued not via a PADD, but in a specially replicated physical edition made from real simulated paper. This means that the next time we encounter a power-draining space anomaly, sentient computer virus, or a plain old quantum filament, you'll still be able to rely on your trusty handbook.

And to make it extra special, we have been given an exclusive, especially written essay on the importance of the Prime Directive, by none other than Admiral Picard himself!

With the knowledge it gives you, you too might rise through the ranks, achieving your dream of becoming a bridge officer, or maybe even your own command…

It's warp time!

BOIMLER:
I feel like I could have been mentioned by name here. I mean, it's no big deal. No, it's not important. Never mind.

FREEMAN:
This is very impressive Lieutenant. How did you swing it?

BOIMLER:
Oh… you know. I've got contacts. Of course, I'm still waiting to receive the final wording but it's going to be here very soon!

LIEUTENANT JUNIOR GRADE BECKETT MARINER

BOIMLER:
Why are you doing this? I asked you to help with the handbook and you said no.

MARINER:
Yeah but the way you said it made it sound all... Boimlery. I'm going to make it more *Mariner-esque*.

BOIMLER:
Okay, but really, how do you think you're going to get away with this? Remember what happened when you went to that reporter behind your mom's back?

MARINER:
I saved the ship and everyone kept apologizing to me for three weeks?

BOIMLER:
Bad example. But what do you think the captain's going to do when she reads this?

MARINER:
That's what you're worried about? Oh Bradward. Poor, simple Bradward. Do you really believe my mom is going to read past her own foreword?

FREEMAN:
Beckett, come to my ready room. *Now.*

BOIMLER:
Not what a *cha'DIch* is.

BOIMLER:
You guessed my password, that's not exactly "hacking."

MARINER:
Well "ZebulonSisters4Eva" was hardly difficult to guess.

BOIMLER:
It's music you can bop to but it also has heart!

BOIMLER:
They aren't buttons they're glowing icons on touch screens

What's up my *cha'DIches*?

Lieutenant Junior Grade Beckett Mariner here, spitting truths and inviting you into that most noble order of Starfleet, the Lower Decks.

The Lower Decks have always been here. We were there in the TOS* era, the TNG** era, and way back in the ENT*** era. In any history book where you see some brave captain leading their ship into the unknown, you better *know* that we are right there behind them, serving them their coffee, handing them their PADDs, cleaning out their replicator nozzles, lubing their turbo lifts, and getting jobs that take ten hours done in two because the chief engineer wants to be "a miracle worker."

The captain might want this handbook updated to add some new items to the contraband list, or remove some of the more, ahem, "problematic" elements of the Ferengi cultural guide now we're all best buds with Grand Nagus Rom, but I have hacked my way in here and I will be giving you the unvarnished, Iyaaran warts and all view of life on the LD.

You want your own command? You want to spend your time filing reports, sucking up to snooty alien diplomats, and dealing with complex moral dilemmas where *whatever you choose*, you will be forced to look sadly out of your Ready Room window afterwards?

Or do you want to be where the action is? Pushing buttons, poking strange alien rocks, sticking our faces in front of strange slimy eggs and seeing what jumps out?

I am your guide, your mentor, your cosmic koala, and I will be here adding my unique and valuable perspective to the proceedings; the truth behind the truth.

LOWER DECKS!

*Those Old Scientists.

** Those Newer Guys.

*** Earth's Newbie Travelers.

COMMANDER JACK RANSOM

MEET YOUR FIRST OFFICER

by Commander Jack Ransom

97... 98... 99... Oh hey! I didn't see you there. I was just doing some lifts. You see, I believe that a body is like a starship crew – you must always be working to keep it in shape. Whether you are working the biceps of the security department, the deltoids of the science department, the abs of the ops crew, or of course, those ever-reliable quadriceps down in engineering, I am here to help you all be in the best shape you can be – and I never skip leg day.

I want you to think of me less as your commander or first officer, and more as a friend whose orders you follow without question. I am a facilitator – facilitating you in carrying out the captain's instructions by telling you what they are.

But I also want to be approachable. If you have any problem, no matter how small, I want you to feel like you can come and speak to me while I'm lifting free weights in my office, or on the equipment at the gym, or in the holodeck when I'm practicing my double-fisted punch, or down in cetacean ops doing lengths with my besties. No matter what kind of workout I'm doing, I will be happy to stop and listen to any issues you have and let you know if they are worth my time (Apart from Lieutenant Commander Steve Stevens, as previously discussed, I would still prefer it if you contact me in writing first).

Because Starfleet is like the round table of Camelot, where we are all equal, even if I am sitting at the right hand of King Arthur in a slightly cooler looking chair.

MARINER:
Seriously? Is he actually pretending we interrupted him working out? In writing? Does Ransom not know how books work?

APPRECIATE YOUR FIRST OFFICER

by Lieutenant Commander Steve Stevens

You don't know how lucky you are to serve under the best first officer in the fleet, Commander Jack Ransom! This guy is a hero, a goddamned hero. He's a fighter, a thinker, a leader, at one time he was an actual *god* (although admittedly that did get a little out of hand). It's an honor, a *privilege* to follow this man into battle, and every one of his orders is a gift that you should thank your lucky stars you get to carry out. But you should also know that no matter how well you serve him, and what dangers you and he may face together on strange new worlds, you will *never* approach the sacred bond that he and I will always share.

MARINER:
Why did you ask
Stevens to write this?

BOIMLER:
I... didn't. I just opened the
manuscript one day and
found he'd added this whole
spread behind my back.

MARINER:
Editing your manuscript
behind your back?!
For shame!

NO SMALL PARTS!

THE MENIAL TASKS THAT ARE ESSENTIAL TO KEEPING THE *CERRITOS* SHIP SHAPE!

by Commander Jack Ransom

As first officer, my job comprises a number of critical duties - advising the captain, leading away missions, handing out the awards on Captain Freeman Day. But while not all the duties aboard the *Cerritos* come with that much authority or excitement, they are all critical to the smooth running of the ship.

Now some might ask, why do we even still have these jobs? Couldn't we automate them? To which I say, sure, we could, but that's not in line with the adventurous spirit of the enlightened 24th century explorer. If you're going to automate carbon filter maintenance, then why not automate scanning for life forms? Or being first officer? And then all a sudden, BAM! You've got yourself another *Texas*-class or M-5 Computer scenario, and then we might as well not bother going into space in the first place.

These duties can also provide junior officers with a much needed opportunity for reflection upon the importance of discipline and respect for the chain of command.

MARINER:
Are they though? We can use lasers and forcefields to create non-sentient humanoids that carry out our every whim. We can reduce matter to energy then rearrange it on the fly to whatever form we wish.

MARINER:
You know why we have these jobs? Ransom likes there to be a punishment detail he can threaten junior officers with.

MARINER:
See! Do you see?! He admits it! *HE ADMITS IT!*

EMPTYING THE HOLODECK BIOFILTERS

The holodeck allows us to create any place, any time, any scenario you can imagine, and when you are done, everything that was manifested can be reduced to a collection of 1s and 0s in the ship's computer core.

But while the holodeck program itself is nothing but a combination of light and energy fields, that's not all you will find in the holodeck. Those who use the holodeck will often leave various kinds of… organic residue. While most of this residue can be easily recycled, many crew are reluctant to allow certain substances to be broken down and recombined to form our food, clothes or hair products. Fluids of that type are efficiently gathered up and stored away in canisters discreetly stowed behind the wall paneling. These canisters fill up with surprising, some might say *alarming* speed, and must be regularly changed by junior officers who will transfer the filled canisters to our auxiliary matter recombinator.

MARINER:
Right, let's ignore for now the fact that we could just beam those canisters out. The key to surviving this job is to *not think about any part of it.* What's in the canisters? *Do not think about it.* Why is there so much of it? *Do not think about it.* Why do the supposedly airtight canisters smell so strong, and by the way, what is that smell? *Do not think about it.* And what happens to all these canisters of organic sludge anyway? *Do. Not. Think. About. It. Ever.*

DIPLOMAT CONCIERGE

On second contact and other diplomatic missions, it's not uncommon for the *Cerritos* to play host to alien dignitaries. Entertaining and engaging with such figures is one of the great privileges of being a senior officer on a Federation ship.

However, sometimes senior officers may be otherwise occupied by a shipboard emergency or the other dignitaries on board that we have to keep a secret because of their centuries long blood feud with the first ones.

Alternatively, we might think a junior officer can benefit from the diplomatic experience. In that case, you must see to it that our guest is provided the appropriate atmospheric settings, ensure the right precautions are taken against e.g. their telepathic field manifesting their nightmares as physical reality, and, most importantly, keep their drinks filled.

MARINER:
Senior officers love nothing more than talking to an alien in a massive frilly gown with a really big hat, so if someone has tried to palm this job off on you then you know that this "guest" is going to be a *nightmare*.

First, do not go alone! You don't just need company, you need *witnesses*. I swear one in every three ambassadors considers saying "Hello" to be a war crime, and the rest turn up assassinated when, conveniently, you're the only person in their quarters.

CARBON FILTER MAINTENANCE

MARINER:

It's scraping carbon off of slightly harder carbon. One of the biggest wastes of time on this ship. Still, if you piss off the wrong person and land this duty, the best tool for the job is a Type 2 phaser on setting number 4. To pass the time, get some of your crew around and compete to see who can scrape the most carbon. Snap! The job's a game!

As someone who has graduated from Starfleet Academy, and at the very least completed the mandatory module on remedial ship functions, you obviously don't need me to explain how important the carbon filters are. Without those carbon filters, filtering all that carbon, the *Cerritos* wouldn't get very far at all.

That's why it's important that the carbon is removed from the carbon filter to allow it to filter carbon properly.

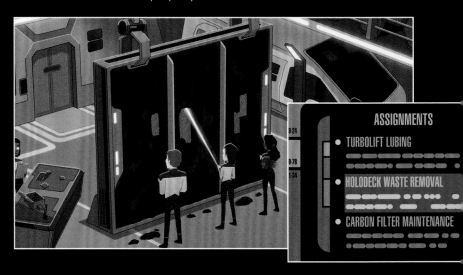

ASSIGNMENTS

- TURBOLIFT LUBING
- HOLODECK WASTE REMOVAL
- CARBON FILTER MAINTENANCE

MARINER:

To lube the turbolifts and survive, you've got to do two things.

One: Put up some signs. Lots and lots of signs. Clearly worded, brightly colored signs that say "Turbolift out of use," "Do not use," "Stay out of this turbolift" etc.

Two: Know that nobody on this ship ever actually *reads* those signs, so be ready to dig your nails into the roof of your turbolift as it rockets through a complex network of oddly spacious lift shafts.

TURBOLIFT LUBING

The turbolifts are the glue that binds the *Cerritos* together. Without them, we would all spend much less time engaged in the vital work of keeping the ship running, and much more time running up and down stairs. Am I right?!

But to keep those elevators running smoothly along their tracks, we need to regularly apply a sophisticated nanobead infused lubricant gel to the lifts' runners, ensuring a smooth ride for everyone!

ANOMALY CONSOLIDATION DUTY

While the *Cerritos*'s primary mission is one of second contact and support, we are still ultimately on a mission of exploration, and you don't explore without coming across things you don't understand. In our travels we pick up new life forms, mysterious artifacts, samples of new states of matter, or previously unencountered subatomic particles.

And sooner or later, all that stuff needs filing. Obviously the senior officers would do this ourselves, but we're too busy finding more strange anomalous objects and substances, so we really appreciate those on the lower decks picking up the slack here.

Still, a proactive, go-getting young officer will find it a great opportunity to review the scientific mysteries the *Cerritos* has encountered, and maybe make some discoveries of their own…

MARINER:
Anomaly Consolidation Day is the *worst*.

CHIEF MEDICAL OFFICER
DR T'ANA

MEDICAL EVALUATION

by Chief Medical Officer Dr. T'Ana

Welcome aboard, fresh meat. You are now part of the crew of the *Cerritos*, which means it's my unpleasant duty to keep you alive.

My sickbay is one of the first places you will visit on the *Cerritos*, before you've dumped your duffel bag on your bunk, but after Commander Ransom has asked you to guess how much he can bench press.

Now one of the junior officers has asked me to write an introduction for this little pamphlet, which I was happy to do because it's not like the ship's chief medical officer doesn't have lots of real work, but then I figured, hey, if I can use this to cover the info I normally have to go through during crew onboarding, it could save me actual hours that I could use for classifying biological samples, doing research, and, what the hell, maybe even treating the odd patient. So, read this, remember it, fill out the medical history form and drop it off in my office when I'm not there.

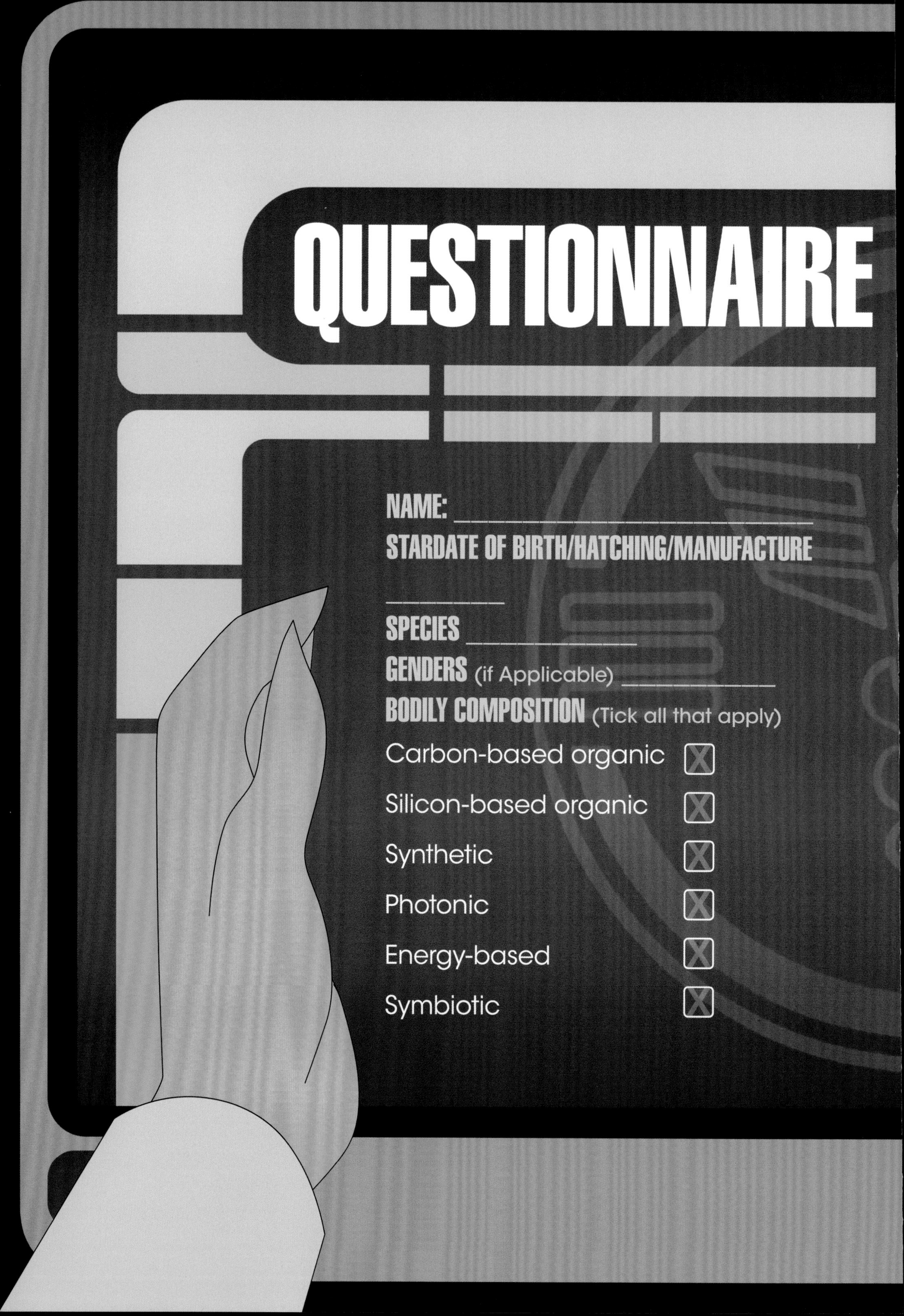

QUESTIONNAIRE

NAME: _____

STARDATE OF BIRTH/HATCHING/MANUFACTURE

_____

SPECIES _____

GENDERS (if Applicable) _____

BODILY COMPOSITION (Tick all that apply)

Carbon-based organic [X]

Silicon-based organic [X]

Synthetic [X]

Photonic [X]

Energy-based [X]

Symbiotic [X]

MEDICAL HISTORY

BLOOD TYPE (acidic, gaseous etc.) _____

NEXT OF KIN _____

CLOSEST LIVING RELATIVE/TRANSPORTER CLONE

_____ _____

Are you indigenous to this time period, timeline, universe, and quantum reality?

Yes ☒ No ☒

If "No," please explain _____

_____

Pre-existing conditions, ailments, injuries, transporter accidents, infestations, deaths etc. _____

_____

_____

_____

_____

_____

_____

DR. T'ANA'S

Do you know why most life evolves on planets rather than in space? It's because space kills things, and it is going to try and kill you. This means that once you board the *Cerritos* it probably won't be long before you turn up on my examination table, which is why I get (Bleep)ed off when I end up with patients arriving in my sickbay with a case of terminal stupidity.

So if you don't want a dose of my very strong personal opinions along with your tissue regeneration, you will not injure yourself breaking any of the following rules:

1. ONLY PLAY SPORTS INVENTED BY YOUR OWN SPECIES

The Federation has hundreds of member species, each with their own in-built biological strengths and vulnerabilities. The games they invent are designed to cater to those limitations. This is why Klingon sports award points for stab wounds and blunt force head injuries, while Human sports involve kicking a ball or, if they are wearing enough protective gear, carrying one.

Oh, and on a related note, your doctor can always tell when your "sports" injury comes from sex with a species that likes it rougher than yours.

Always.

2. DON'T TURN THE HOLODECK SAFETIES OFF

That's why they're called "safeties," dumbass. I only have time to regrow so many severed hands, I refuse to believe the holodecks "break down" as much as some officers claim, and I happen to know that's not even how the plot of *Little Women* goes anyway.

BOIMLER:
What does "(Bleep)" even mean?

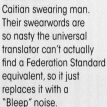

MARINER:
Caitian swearing man. Their swearwords are so nasty the universal translator can't actually find a Federation Standard equivalent, so it just replaces it with a "Bleep" noise.

SICKBAY
HEALTH GUIDELINES

3. WHEN YOU BEAM UP NOVEL BIOLOGICAL SAMPLES, TRAVEL SEPARATELY

The ship's transporter is a truly amazing piece of technology that analyzes the position of every atom of your DNA, as well as everything else about your person, so that it can disassemble you and reassemble you at your destination. It can even identify any potential pathogens or infections and filter them out on the fly while it rebuilds you.

It can do this so flawlessly because we have centuries of pre-existing data on how a transporter pattern is supposed to look. If you beam up with something that those scanners have never seen before you are going to throw out all its calculations. That's how you end up with mutations, transporter psychosis, Tuvixes and God knows what else.

4. NO KLINGON WEAPONRY

I don't know where people are getting these from but I have lost count of the bat'leth and d'k tahg injuries I've had to shine a light at. Where do they come from? We don't even go near Klingon space!

5. ATTEND YOUR PHYSICAL

We have the technology to scan your entire body, immediately identifying anything wrong with you and fixing it before it becomes a problem, and we do this by waving a tricorder at you. It takes literally five seconds. Why wouldn't you?

6. DO NOT QUOTE ANY OF THESE RULES TO DR. T'ANA

I'm a doctor, I know better than you, so do as I say, not what I do. Anyone who thinks they can (Bleep)ing call me out for not obeying any of these rules will soon need medical attention.

BOIMLER:
Don't say pussycat, don't say pussycat, don't say pussycat…

LIEUTENANT JUNIOR GRADE
D'VANA TENDI

A GUIDE TO STAYING ON DR. T'ANA'S GOOD SIDE

Dr. T'Ana has a bit of a scary reputation among some of the crew, but the truth is, once you get to know her she can be a really good friend. You just need to know how to relate to her on her own level. Here are the tips I've learned for getting along in sickbay.

1. Stand up for yourself. Dr. T'Ana appreciates a bit of assertiveness and the ability to stand your ground. Don't be afraid to speak your mind and voice professional disagreement when necessary.

2. Do everything she says.

3. Blink slowly at her. I don't know why but this works really well.

4. If she has Shaxs in her office, take a long walk around the deck.

5. Don't try too hard. She hates it when junior officers follow her around, asking for tips on how to be a better medical officer and staring intently at her while she's treating patients so that you can learn. I know that now. Instead, simply do your work and let her come to you when she's ready.

6. Never ask how she lost her tail.

7. Bringing her the occasional glass of milk doesn't hurt!

MARINER:
How come Tendi gets to write in your handbook?

BOIMLER:
I asked her to send me something. She's the only junior officer to get through her first week with Dr. T'Ana without crying.

SHAXS'S SECURITY BRIEFING

by Lieutenant Shaxs

The universe is a dangerous place, full of unimaginable terrors and critical threats. Sheliak, Qs, Pah-wraiths, Pakleds, skins of evil, Cardassians, and worse. As the chief security officer of the *Cerritos*, the ship I love so much, it is my duty and pleasure to protect this ship, its crew, and their emotional wellbeing from those threats.

Now it's important to remember that Starfleet is first and foremost a scientific, humanitarian, and diplomatic organization devoted to the concepts of peaceful coexistence, understanding, exploration, and research, with violence only ever deployed as a last resort.

BOIMLER:
Umm. We've made peace with the Cardassians, can we say that?

W.O.R.F.

As chief security officer, my job is to guide the captain to that last resort as quickly and efficiently as possible. To do this, I like to employ my patented persuasive method, "WORF." Let me talk you through it.

W: "WE SHOULD LAUNCH QUANTUM TORPEDOES."

You have encountered something new. Maybe it's an unidentified ship. Maybe it's a spatial anomaly. Maybe it's a spaceborne telepathic plant that makes everyone feel things. Whatever it is, the captain's first step will be to ask key members of her bridge crew for input and tactical analysis. This is the ideal time to suggest that you launch quantum torpedoes to neutralize a potential threat.

O: ". . . OR WE COULD LAUNCH QUANTUM TORPEDOES?"

While your opening gambit was persuasive, it's possible the captain wants to try other options. She may scan the new phenomenon. She might want to attempt to open a communications channel. She may even have beamed over an away team to investigate. When none of these approaches yield results, it is time to once again draw your captain's attention to your elegant and effective solution.

R: "RETALIATE WITH QUANTUM TORPEDOES!"

By now the captain will have wasted valuable time, and the new phenomenon will have revealed itself to be the threat it always was. Maybe the ship opens fire. Maybe the spatial anomaly starts sapping the ship's power. Maybe the telepathic plant makes you feel bad things, things you haven't let yourself feel in such a long time. However the threat manifests, there is only one way to respond: with a show of force. Alert your captain to this at first opportunity.

F: "FIRE QUANTUM TORPEDOES!"

If you have taken the steps above, your captain should now be giving you the order to fire torpedoes. Congratulations! The threat is neutralized!

Of course, not every problem can be solved by firing quantum torpedoes. This technique can also be used to persuade the captain to fire photon torpedoes, fire phasers, approach at ramming speed, or eject the warp core.

THE SECURITY OFFICER'S FIELD GUIDE:
A TAMARIAN GLOSSARY

by Lieutenant Junior Grade Kayshon

The word "Picard and Dathon at El-Adrel" is carved into the walls of the Lexicographers' Temple on Tamar. That word will be uttered by the children of the children of the children of Tamar. It tells how we came to understand the Federation. And yet, Kadir beneath Mo Moteh! Making your universal translators understand me can be *quite* the beast at Tanagra.

Not all our words are carved in the Lexicographer's temple.
Some words are Atash, her axe worn. Tools to be used, and discarded. "Slang."

Those Children of Tamar who have joined Starfleet may be Ubaya of crossroads, at Lungha. Between two cultures. We can craft our own words.
Atash, her rock sharpened.

To avoid Zima at Anzor, I have asked Lieutenant Junior Grade Boimler to help me translate some phrases from Tamarian Starfleet officers into Federation Standard. Temba, his arms wide!

"Ensign Grayson, her head purple"
– Do not try new alien foods that have not been properly bioscanned.

"Transporter Room 4, when his head hatched"
– Someone will have to clean this up.

"The hands of Lieutenant Henry, their thumbs missing"
– When dealing with alien cultures, remember that usually harmless gestures or greetings may be interpreted differently.

"The spear in Ensign Vendome's shoulder"
– Advanced technology will not always protect you.

"Kira at Bashir"
– To try to get someone to stop telling an overlong story.

"Ensign Baldwin, in the Jefferies tubes"
– Do not enter a situation you do not know how to escape from.

"Ensign MacReady phasered, her duplicate escaped"
– If a shapeshifting predator has infiltrated the crew, quickly try to establish a code word to avoid tragic mistakes.

"Lieutenant Mallory, when the rock explodes"
– Sometimes bad things will just happen to you for no apparent reason.

LIEUTENANT JUNIOR GRADE KAYSHON

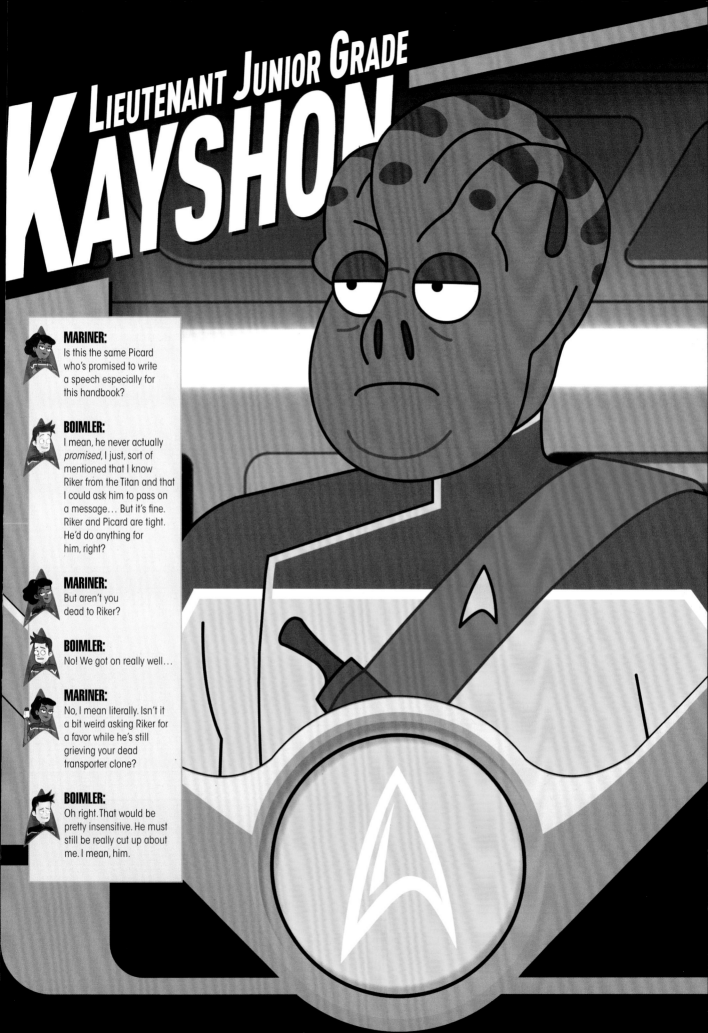

MARINER:
Is this the same Picard who's promised to write a speech especially for this handbook?

BOIMLER:
I mean, he never actually *promised*, I just, sort of mentioned that I know Riker from the Titan and that I could ask him to pass on a message... But it's fine. Riker and Picard are tight. He'd do anything for him, right?

MARINER:
But aren't you dead to Riker?

BOIMLER:
No! We got on really well...

MARINER:
No, I mean literally. Isn't it a bit weird asking Riker for a favor while he's still grieving your dead transporter clone?

BOIMLER:
Oh right. That would be pretty insensitive. He must still be really cut up about me. I mean, him.

CREW NOTICE: UPDATED
CONTRABAND LIST

THE FOLLOWING ITEMS ARE PROHIBITED ABOARD THE *U.S.S. CERRITOS*.

KTARIAN VIDEOGAMES

TRIBBLES

KLINGON WEAPONRY

REGALIAN LIQUID CRYSTAL

MARINER:
If you know what I mean...

VULCAN WEAPONRY
(UNLESS WITH SPECIAL DISPENSATION)

TRICORDERS WITH THE BLUE STRIPE
(UNLESS OFFICIALLY ISSUED)

THE BEST PLACES TO HIDE CONTRABAND ABOARD THE *CERRITOS* ARE AS FOLLOWS:

Literally any Jefferies Tube.

The closet on the captain's yacht.

On the roof of Turbolift 5 (you might have to call a few lifts to get the right one).

Below the hydroponics bay among the Tamarian defrin root.

In the hold of the ancient pirate sailing ship constantly running in Holodeck 4 (make sure to keep the room booked).

The rubber ducky room.

The medical transporter buffer.

The pocket dimension they accidentally created in Astrophysics Lab 2.

Under Boimler's mattress

BOIMLER:
Wait, what?

MARINER:
What?

ROMULAN ALE

ENOLIAN PICE WINE

ANCIENT MASKS OF ANY KIND

LIEUTENANT COMMANDER
ANDY BILLUPS

ENGINEERING 101

by Lieutenant Commander Andy Billups

Welcome to Engineering, where we put the "go" into "to boldly go!" Now believe it or not, a lot of people can find Starfleet engineers intimidating, complaining that we always talk in impenetrable technical jargon. But personally, I *like* technical jargon.

What some might call "meaningless technobabble" or "are you making those words up as you go along?" is simply an operative shorthand to allow trained professionals to communicate in the most precise and efficient way.

You see, I grew up on Hysperia, a Human colony that on a cultural, aesthetic and yes, linguistic level, leans towards the mythic and magical. So I find it a genuine relief to call a space matrix restoration coil a space matrix restoration coil and not, ahem, "the Phoenix Serpent's Web."

BOIMLER:
Yeah, we've been asked to remove jokes like this.

However, it's easy to understand how officers in less technically rigorous departments, like Command, Security, or Ops, might feel daunted by some of our terminology. So to bring everyone up to speed (warp speed, ha ha!) allow me to explain the workings of the warp core in terms so simple even a Pakled could understand!

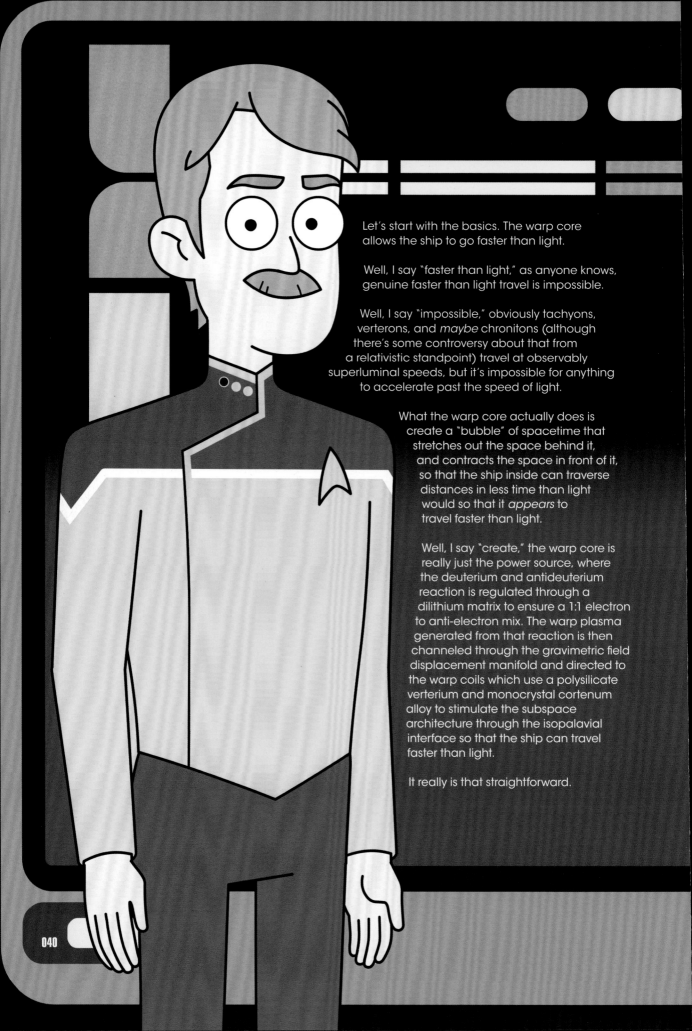

Let's start with the basics. The warp core allows the ship to go faster than light.

Well, I say "faster than light," as anyone knows, genuine faster than light travel is impossible.

Well, I say "impossible," obviously tachyons, verterons, and *maybe* chronitons (although there's some controversy about that from a relativistic standpoint) travel at observably superluminal speeds, but it's impossible for anything to accelerate past the speed of light.

What the warp core actually does is create a "bubble" of spacetime that stretches out the space behind it, and contracts the space in front of it, so that the ship inside can traverse distances in less time than light would so that it *appears* to travel faster than light.

Well, I say "create," the warp core is really just the power source, where the deuterium and antideuterium reaction is regulated through a dilithium matrix to ensure a 1:1 electron to anti-electron mix. The warp plasma generated from that reaction is then channeled through the gravimetric field displacement manifold and directed to the warp coils which use a polysilicate verterium and monocrystal cortenum alloy to stimulate the subspace architecture through the isopalavial interface so that the ship can travel faster than light.

It really is that straightforward.

LIEUTENANT JUNIOR GRADE
SAMANTHAN RUTHERFORD

Hi there, new ensigns! I once heard an old Earth saying that a poor workman blames his tools. But now that we don't use money, nobody's poor, so we can all use better tools! Of course, while we can all replicate anything we need, every starship that's been in space for a while will have its own idiosyncrasies regarding what equipment is in stock or stored in the replicator database. So if you're new to the *Cerritos*, it might be worth refamiliarizing yourself with the standard toolset. And who doesn't enjoy looking at tools?

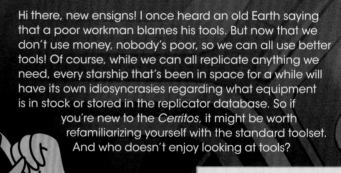

MARINER:
Rutherford?! You invited *Rutherford* to write in this? Is this just because you're roomies?

BOIMLER:
Not at all! He has specialized knowledge! Boimler *cannot* be bought.

MARINER:
I have specialized knowledge! You won't believe how much specialized knowledge I have! I have specialized knowledge on everything!

THE ENGINEER'S TOOLBOX!

COMBADGE

Combadges were introduced in the early 24th century to prevent away missions from accidentally leaving their communicators behind and inadvertently redirecting the technological development of pre-warp planets. But I like to think of them as the toolbox that's always with you! In a pinch, there are few engineering problems you can't solve with a careful application of gold, microfilament, silicon, beryllium, and carbon-70, a subspace transistor with 500km range, and a power cell that is small, but packs a punch!

With a bit of rewiring, your trusty combadge can become a distress beacon, a small, short-lived forcefield generator, lock pick, or improvised explosive device!

T88

The T88! The *Sovereign* class of diagnostic tools! Some say it's ideal for medical diagnostic applications, but it's clearly more suited to engineering purposes. It's efficient, accurate, and has a soft grip on the handle that makes it comfortable to hold for hours!

D53

Forget about the D53. After you've tried the T88, the D53 is trash. The T88 makes the D53 look like the T72. I'm not kidding!

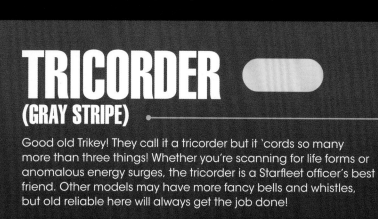

TRICORDER
(GRAY STRIPE)

Good old Trikey! They call it a tricorder but it 'cords so many more than three things! Whether you're scanning for life forms or anomalous energy surges, the tricorder is a Starfleet officer's best friend. Other models may have more fancy bells and whistles, but old reliable here will always get the job done!

MARINER:
Also on a long shift it makes a neat glove puppet! Mr. Tricorder *always* goes down a storm.

TRICORDER
(BURNT ORANGE STRIPE)

The rumor is that only two prototypes of this tricorder were ever produced, and one was issued to a ship that then got lost in the Gamma Quadrant. This tricorder utilizes a positronic mesh that allows it to take readings on how computers are *feeling*. What's more, the burnt orange stripe really pops against the gold of my uniform!

TRICORDER
(PURPLE STRIPE)

The purple stripe tricorder! This model is not yet rolled out across the whole Starfleet, but it boasts better efficiency, deeper scan range, smoother button actions, and all new sound effects! And it's purple!

MARINER:
Although it has to be said, when you try to do Mr. Tricorder with these ones they look grouchy.

TRICORDER
(CYAN STRIPE)

This cheeky little number was rolled out across some *Obena*-class ships, but was later recalled due to an overly intuitive heuristic analysis framework, but if you like to play it a bit fast and loose with your statistical curves, the cyan stripe Tricorder can offer a fresh angle on things.

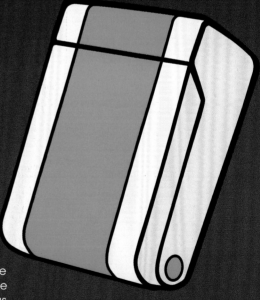

TYPE II PHASER

Most people might think of the Type II Phaser as a simple defensive weapon, but here in engineering all we see is a tool for directing focused beams of energy, and we can think of *all sorts* of uses for that! By modifying the settings and tweaking the beam spread, the phaser can become a precision engineering tool.

You can use it to heat up rocks on a cold planet, to do a bit of light welding, laser cutting, or even carbon filter maintenance.

MARINER:
You can also use the Type II phaser to warm your drink, burn the phrase "Lower Decks 4 Life!" into hard-to-reach places, and to vaporize shipping containers and remove any evidence of your covert "Art supplies to alien schools" initiative.

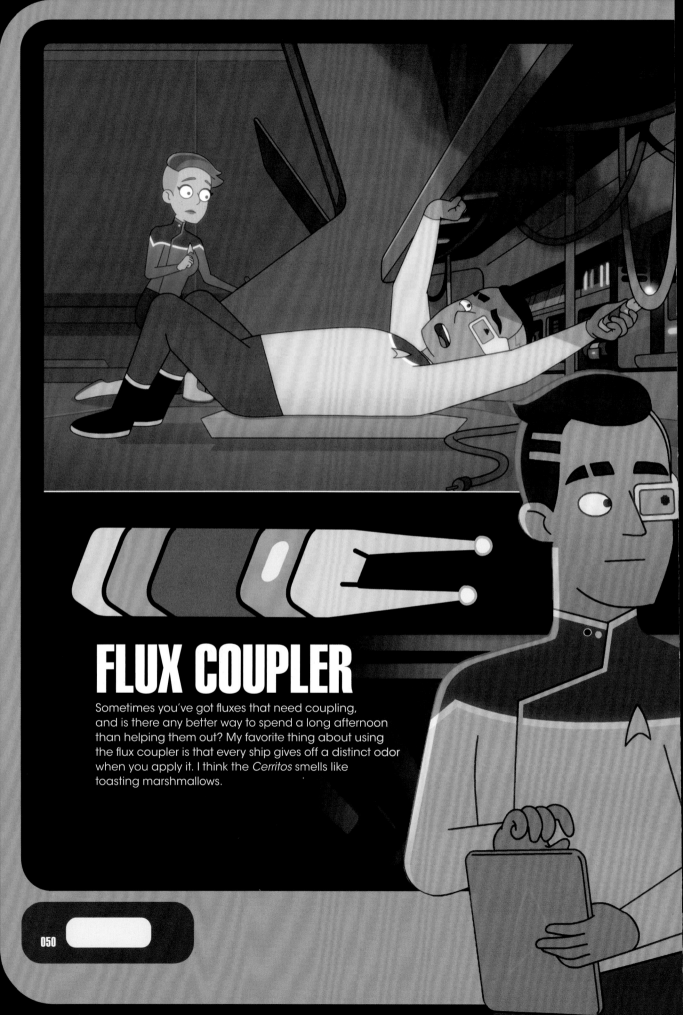

FLUX COUPLER

Sometimes you've got fluxes that need coupling, and is there any better way to spend a long afternoon than helping them out? My favorite thing about using the flux coupler is that every ship gives off a distinct odor when you apply it. I think the *Cerritos* smells like toasting marshmallows.

HYPERSPANNER

Oh hyperspanner! Is there anything you can't do? Yes, lots of things, that's why you have to be careful not to get it confused with the isolinear spanner, the microspanner, or (Ha!) the interphasic coil spanner!

TUCKER TUBES

As invented by Charles "Trip" Tucker, chief engineer aboard the second starship *Enterprise*!

BILLUPS TUBES

Developed by Ensign Livik. Yes, it has one entire tube more than the Tucker Tubes without triggering a Heisenberg collapse, but does it have *heart*?

BOIMLER:
Second?

RUTHERFORD:
After the XCV-330!

BOIMLER:
The XCV-330 doesn't count! It didn't have nacelles! The NX-01 was the first!

MARINER:
Please, the NX-01 wasn't even Federation. Either go 1701 or go home!

HI THERE!
I'M BADGEY 2.0!
CAN I TEACH YOU A LESSON?

I was created as a holodeck program to help junior officers navigate complex or difficult scenarios by extrapolating best practice from data in old Starfleet logs.

Unfortunately, development on my program ceased when I got a bit… murderous.

However, I can't try to kill you from the pages of a printed book, can I? So Samanthan Rutherford, my creator, has extracted my decision tree algorithms to be displayed on the page, allowing you to learn from me in perfect safety! Yay!

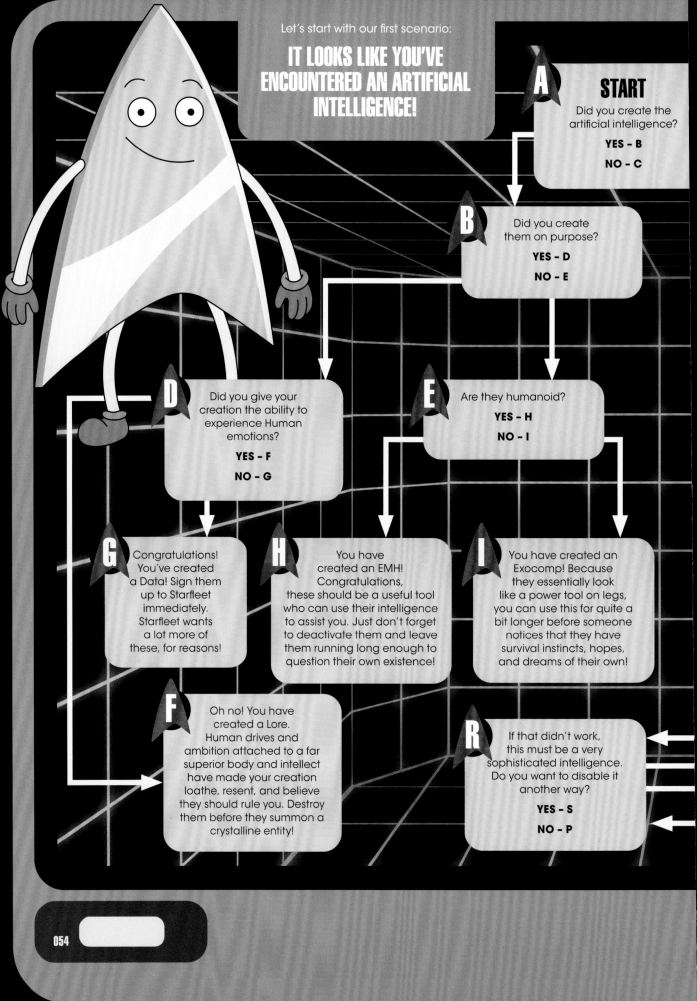

Let's start with our first scenario:

IT LOOKS LIKE YOU'VE ENCOUNTERED AN ARTIFICIAL INTELLIGENCE!

A START
Did you create the artificial intelligence?
YES – B
NO – C

B
Did you create them on purpose?
YES – D
NO – E

D
Did you give your creation the ability to experience Human emotions?
YES – F
NO – G

E
Are they humanoid?
YES – H
NO – I

G
Congratulations! You've created a Data! Sign them up to Starfleet immediately. Starfleet wants a lot more of these, for reasons!

H
You have created an EMH! Congratulations, these should be a useful tool who can use their intelligence to assist you. Just don't forget to deactivate them and leave them running long enough to question their own existence!

I
You have created an Exocomp! Because they essentially look like a power tool on legs, you can use this for quite a bit longer before someone notices that they have survival instincts, hopes, and dreams of their own!

F
Oh no! You have created a Lore. Human drives and ambition attached to a far superior body and intellect have made your creation loathe, resent, and believe they should rule you. Destroy them before they summon a crystalline entity!

R
If that didn't work, this must be a very sophisticated intelligence. Do you want to disable it another way?
YES – S
NO – P

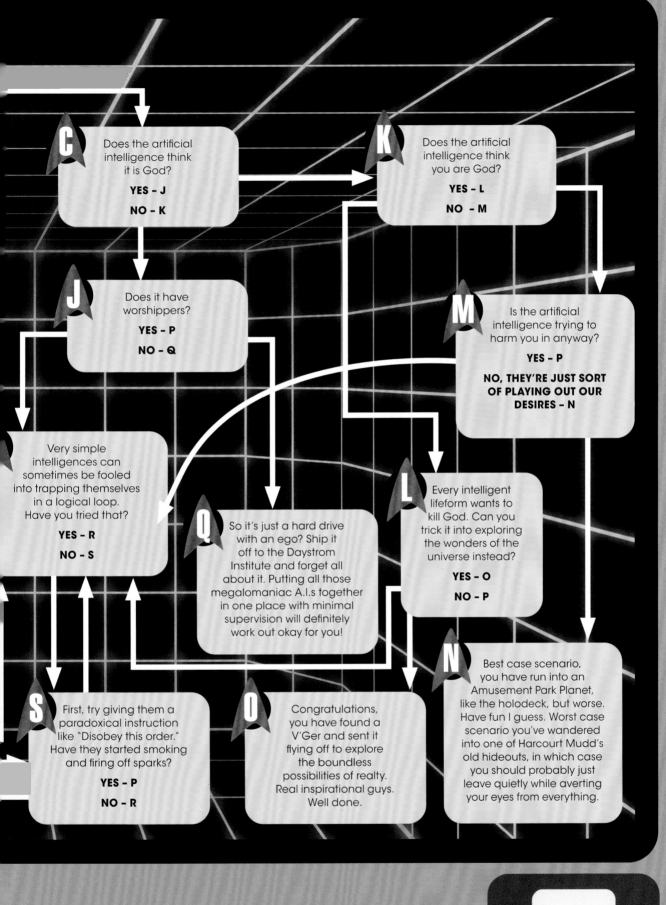

C Does the artificial intelligence think it is God?

YES – J

NO – K

K Does the artificial intelligence think you are God?

YES – L

NO – M

J Does it have worshippers?

YES – P

NO – Q

M Is the artificial intelligence trying to harm you in anyway?

YES – P

NO, THEY'RE JUST SORT OF PLAYING OUT OUR DESIRES – N

Very simple intelligences can sometimes be fooled into trapping themselves in a logical loop. Have you tried that?

YES – R

NO – S

Q So it's just a hard drive with an ego? Ship it off to the Daystrom Institute and forget all about it. Putting all those megalomaniac A.I.s together in one place with minimal supervision will definitely work out okay for you!

L Every intelligent lifeform wants to kill God. Can you trick it into exploring the wonders of the universe instead?

YES – O

NO – P

S First, try giving them a paradoxical instruction like "Disobey this order." Have they started smoking and firing off sparks?

YES – P

NO – R

O Congratulations, you have found a V'Ger and sent it flying off to explore the boundless possibilities of realty. Real inspirational guys. Well done.

N Best case scenario, you have run into an Amusement Park Planet, like the holodeck, but worse. Have fun I guess. Worst case scenario you've wandered into one of Harcourt Mudd's old hideouts, in which case you should probably just leave quietly while averting your eyes from everything.

IN THE BRAIN KITCHEN

WITH YOUR SHIP'S COUNSELLOR!

by Dr. Migleemo

Life on a starship is a lot like eating a large portion of seafood paella. You must chew through many forkfuls of boredom rice, interspersed with the occasional king prawn of terror. Maintaining a healthy mental attitude under such circumstances is a hard taspar egg to crack.

As well as looking after your own wellbeing, it is also essential to pay attention to the relationships and dynamics you have with others, even if your species no longer has interpersonal conflict. While we might be pressed together like sardines, we are not all peas in a pod, and we need to learn how to make our different flavors work together.

Indeed, collectively, *California*-class crews are a Rokeg blood pie of fascinating psychological issues. There are layers to this ship, like tiramisu. On the one hand, to even be part of Starfleet one must be the absolute crème de la crème, and yet sometimes on support ships such as the *Cerritos* we can feel like chopped liver.

We need to make sure that our feelings are processed, like hot dog meat, so that we can handle them fresh off the grill with the bun of our coping mechanisms.

Those coping mechanisms can be as nutritious as a lokar bean quinoa salad or as instantly gratifying but ultimately self-destructive as hasparat from an off-Bajor vendor. But if you find yourself in an emotional pickle, consider me your mental health sommelier.

Because while we are here to explore the outer reaches of the Milky Way, it can be just as rewarding, intimidating, and mysterious to explore the inner depths of your own psyche. The happier, healthy state of mind you can achieve is simply the icing on the cake!

PSYCHOLOGICAL
CASE STUDIES

MARINER:

I don't know who this is supposed to be but it is wrong, wrong, wrong.

Come on Boims, it seems like *everyone* gets to write a chapter of this thing. Just gimme one measly little chapter

BOIMLER:

It's nothing personal, I'm just asking for contributors who can really bring an interesting angle to the handbook.

MARINER:

What like… Picard?

BOIMLER:
What?

MARINER:

Picard. Jean-Luc. I did some archaeology work for him a while ago, remember? If you wanted I could put a word in…

BOIMLER:

I will not be bribed. …Ok, maybe I will.

To demonstrate some of the croutons of difficulty you may find floating in the soup of your mind, I have assembled a small collection of extracts from the psychological profiles I take of the crew. Naturally, these have been fully anonymized to protect their confidentiality.

PATIENT "A"

"…but it must be said that the seniority of her position drives a deep-seated emotional need to control her environment and even the people around her. [Patient A] is prone to micro-management, and she could stand to personally oversee less of the tasks being carried out on-board. She has just informed me that I should change that to 'oversee fewer of the tasks being carried out on-board'."

PATIENT "F"

"[Patient F] shows clear enthusiasm for their work, and is highly motivated to succeed in their field, often at the expense of developing any healthy hobbies or leisure activities. The patient will frequently attempt to avoid social or emotional conflict by seeking out an operational or scientific solution. They show a deep-seated need for approval from their superiors which is often reflected in people-pleasing behavior."

PATIENT "X"

"[Patient X] presents a fascinating case. I have observed she has issues with the authoritative structures and hierarchies of Starfleet, reflecting the relationship difficulties she has with her mother. Her record is a fruit salad of insubordination, and it is clear that she views herself as a rebel and a slacker.

A great deal of [Patient X]'s difficulties come from trying to maintain this self-image, given that it is clear she whole-heartedly supports the philosophy and aims of Starfleet, and has chosen to pursue one of the most challenging and personally taxing careers available in a society where nobody has to work if they don't want to."

MEET THE LOWER DECKS!

by Lieutenant Junior Grade Beckett Mariner

BOIMLER:
Nobody else has ever said this.

MARINER:
That's what makes it unofficial, duh!

Hi! It's me again! Beckett Mariner, the sort of "unofficial leader" of the Lower Deckers, the Ensign's Ensign, if you will.

So by now you've met all the senior staff, the XO, the chief engineer, the chief medical officer, and they have all had a lot to say to you but I am here to tell you now that you can forget *most of it*. The noble ideals of Starfleet, the rules and regulations, the grand missions, that's all upper deck stuff. If there's any of it that you need to know, you can guarantee that a senior officer is going to exposition it at you. The rest of the time, all you need to know is when your shift starts, when your shift ends, who you have to report to, and how to stack crates. That last one is going to come up a lot. What's more, the senior officers have, like, zero object permanence, so as soon as they hand you a PADD and some instructions, you cease to exist to them.

Does that sound depressing? Well it's not! It means that most of the time we have free rein of the ship. When your senior officer gives you a job to do they don't know how long it will take or even probably what it involves, giving you time to chat with your friends, fit in a little buffer time, and hey, maybe even go hang out by the warp core.

BOIMLER:
You're a Lieutenant Junior Grade.

MARINER:
In my *heart,* I am an Ensign!

My point is, you don't need to worry about the senior officers, you need to focus on your fellow scrappy underdogs, the lower deckers! But not all lower deckers are created equal, so pay close attention to which shift you are assigned to.

KNOW YOUR SHIFTS!

ASIF:
Oh ha ha, vampire rules.
Very funny guys!
We're in space!
There *is* no nighttime!

DELTA (THE NIGHT SHIFT)

A few rules for dealing with crewmembers in Delta Shift.

- They only work at night, because sunlight burns them.

- They hate garlic.

- They cannot enter your quarters without your permission.

ASIF:
That's true of anyone!
It would be really rude!
Come on Boimler, are you
going to allow this?

BOIMLER:
I am. Sorry guys, Delta
Shift's weird! There's no
getting around it.

MEET THE DELTA SHIFTER

by Ensign Duval Asif

Delta Shift gets a bad rap, but the truth is night shift is where the real action is! Like one time, this terraforming agent from an alien colony ship infected the *Cerritos*, turning everything into plants and rocks and corals and stuff, and after the crew figured out a way to reverse its effects, Delta Shift woke up and had to search all the Jefferies tubes for leftover roots or moss!

And this other time, we came under attack by the Pakleds, and Moxie nearly fell out of her bunk. Wild times!

GAMMA SHIFT
(UNKNOWN?)

We've never actually met anyone from Gamma Shift. I don't think anyone has. The rumor is that Shaxs has assembled them into his own personal "Hazard Team," an elite force who he sends out on only the most dangerous of away missions.

BOIMLER:
Do they even exist? Should we be including them if no one's ever seen them?

BOIMLER:
Is that true?

MARINER:
Shaxs asked me to put it in and did those big puppy dog eyes. He does have a group of security ensigns he calls "the Hazard Team," but mostly they play laser tag in the holodeck.

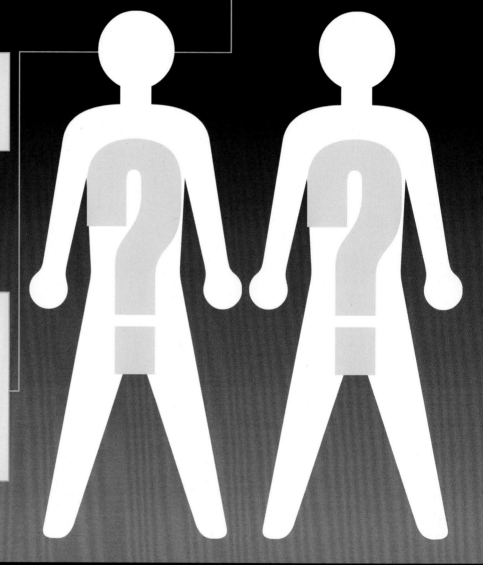

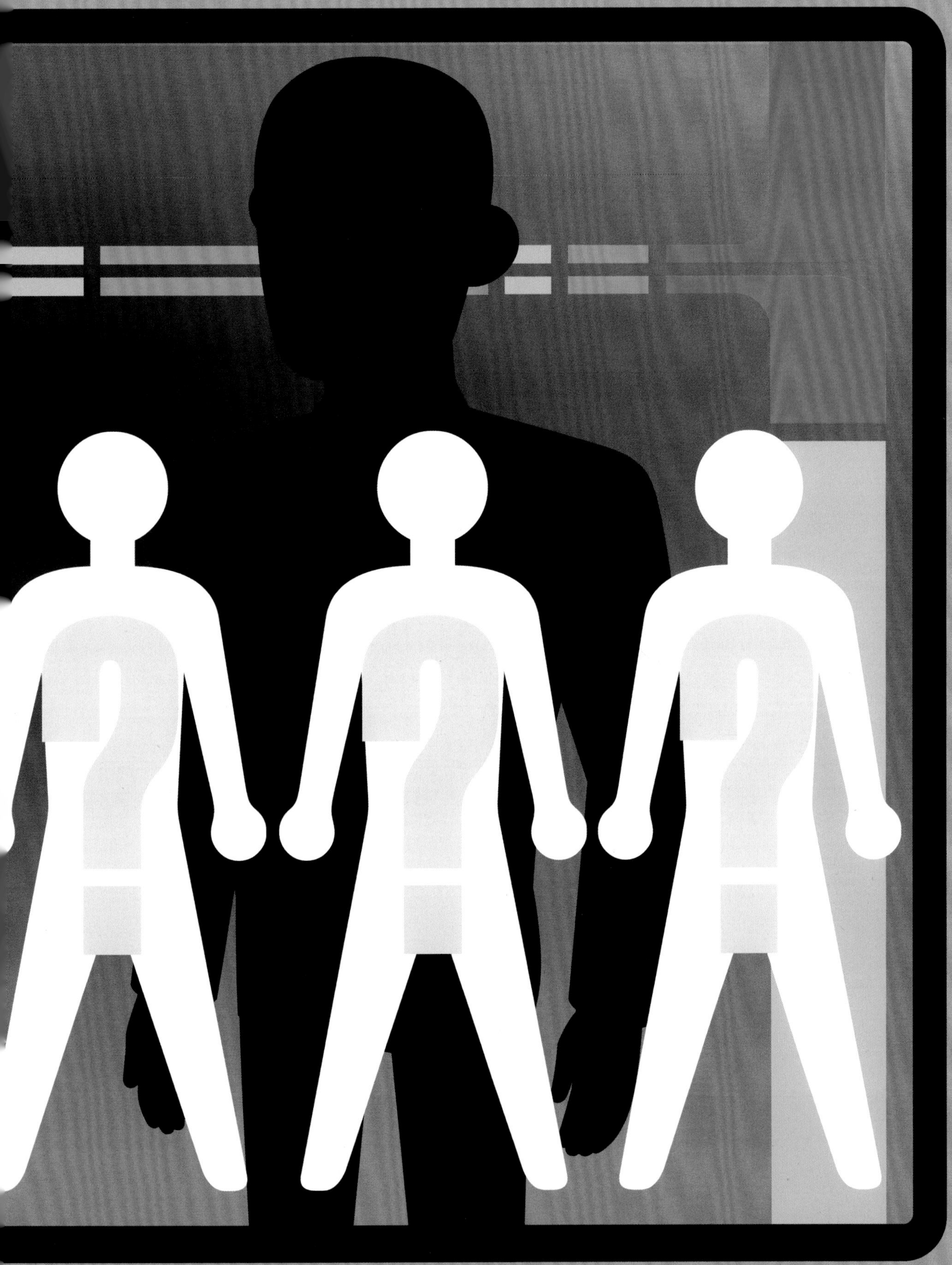

BETA SHIFT
(DAY SHIFT)

With all due modesty, I think it's fair to say that Beta shift is the "main" shift. We're the ones that take the away missions, that handle the big crises, and make the second contacts. The story of the *Cerritos* is, at the end of the day, the story of Beta Shift. As I always say, if it ain't Beta Shift, it ain't canon!

MEET THE BETA SHIFTER

by Ensign Jet Manhaver

Beta Shift is okay I guess. I heard a lot of hype about it when I got transferred from Alpha Shift. I mean, each shift is literally a quarter of the entire crew, y'know? And space doesn't care what the shipboard clock says, so there's always something to do. But I like Beta Shift just fine.

ALPHA SHIFT
(MORNING SHIFT)

The "Early Bird" shift, so quiet we don't even notice them a lot of the time. Who knows what they do that early? Putting out the coasters? Cleaning down all the chairs after Delta Shift's been sitting on them? Mainly, Alpha Shift's job is to clear the runway for Beta Shift to come in and do our thing.

MEET THE ALPHA SHIFTER

by Ensign Sherwyns

Yeah there's always plenty to do during Alpha Shift. Like that one time when we ran into those Borg, that was pretty hairy. Or that invasion from the Mirror Universe. Oh, or there was that time we hit a spatial anomaly that shrank the ship to microscopic size and we got lost in Admiral Jellico's circulatory system. That voyage was pretty fantastic!

But yeah, the important thing is we get everything sorted out and tidied up by the end of the shift.

MARINER:
That's not real.
He's making that up.

BOIMLER:
Almost certainly.

MARINER:
He has to be, right?

BOIMLER:
I mean, it's easy enough to check. We can just look at the ship's logs?

MARINER:
Ummm… No. No. I'm so confident I don't need to check. And neither do you. Let's never check.

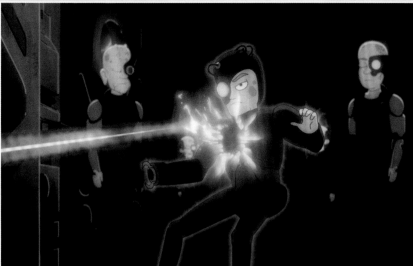

SOCIALS BOARD
U.S.S. CERRITOS
NCC-75567

THE REDSHIRTS
"FEEL INVINCIBLE!"

Are you captain material? Would you like to be? Are you working *in* Starfleet, or *for* Starfleet?

An important networking and training opportunity for ambitious junior officers with their eyes on the prize! We will be holding seminars and workshops on:

- Choosing your pose: Ensign Casey explains how to sit in the captain's chair in a way that is authoritative yet casual
- Ensign Castro leads an inspirational speech improv workshop
- Sartorial maneuvers: Ensign Taylor teaches standing up to greet alien dignitaries without getting your uniform all bunched up
- Engaging catch phrases: Picking the right catch phrase for your command

RECITAL AUDITORIUM 2, MONDAYS, WEDNESDAYS AND THURSDAYS, 1300 HOURS, SHIP TIME.

BOARD GAME CLUB

The best fun you can have on *board* the *Cerritos!* A great place to come and mingle with fellow crew while trying out our extensive boardgame library, including classics such as:

- *Chess* (2D) - for beginners
- *Kal-toh*
- *Terrace*
- *Kadis-kot*
- *Chess* (3D) - for advanced players
- *Chula* (Home edition)
- *Bat'leths & blHnuchs*
- *Stratagema*
- *Chess* (1D)
  - for very advanced players

CERRITOS BAR, TUESDAY EVENINGS, 1800 HOURS, SHIP TIME

BAND MEMBERS WANTED!

Electric violinist seeks:
Anyone to play the other instruments.

CONTACT:
B. Boimler, Deck 11, call by tapping your combadge and saying "Boimler"

SHAKESPEARE SOCIETY

Experience the words of the Bard as they were intended! Join our production of *Much Ado About Nothing*!

- The original text performed as written by Shakespeare himself!
- Period correct costumes for 17th century Messina
- Performed on a traditional stage with no holodeck special effects
- No "reinterpretations"
- Great fun all round!

CARGO BAY 2, ALTERNATE TUESDAYS, 1800 HOURS, SHIP TIME

PARRISES SQUARES
4-A-SIDE FRIENDLIES LEAGUE

Our new league starts next week and we're looking for new players for the Ops, Medical, and Security teams.

REMINDER:

This is a *friendly* league. We are here to have fun and enjoy the game. Set your ion mallets to half power, we don't want a repeat of what happened to Ensign Sherwyns last season.

GYMNASIUM 5, SUNDAYS, 0900 HOURS, SHIP TIME

KLINGON
SHAKESPEARE SOCIETY

⟨Ex⟩perience the *original* words of the ⟨Ba⟩rd as they were *actually* intended! ⟨I⟩n our production of *paghmo' tIn mIS*!

⟨T⟩he original text performed as written ⟨b⟩y Shex'pir himself!
⟨P⟩eriod correct costumes ⟨f⟩or 2nd Dynasty era Mekro'vak
⟨P⟩erformed against the romantic ⟨h⟩olographic backdrop of the ⟨b⟩aH'Hud volcanos
⟨R⟩eal injuries! (A medical officer with a ⟨t⟩issue regenerator will be on stand-by)
⟨A⟩ serious dramatic and academic ⟨e⟩xercise for people not easily taken in ⟨b⟩y Human-centric propaganda

HOLODECK 3, ALTERNATE TUESDAYS, 1800 HOURS, SHIP TIME

GILBERT & SULLIVAN CLUB

- We're probably going to put on *H.M.S. Pinafore* again!
- Come along and join in!
- You won't even have to learn any lyrics as everyone in Starfleet basically knows Gilbert and Sullivan by heart anyway!

CERRITOS BAR, TUESDAY EVENINGS AFTER 2200 HOURS, SHIP TIME

BAJORAN
POTTERY CLASS
with Shaxs

Learn to shape the clay, mold the clay, put all your feelings into the clay, deep, deep into the clay. They can't hurt you from inside the clay.

ACTIVITY ROOM 4, SATURDAYS, 1100 HOURS SHIP TIME

LIEUTENANT JUNIOR GRADE
BRADWARD BOIMLER

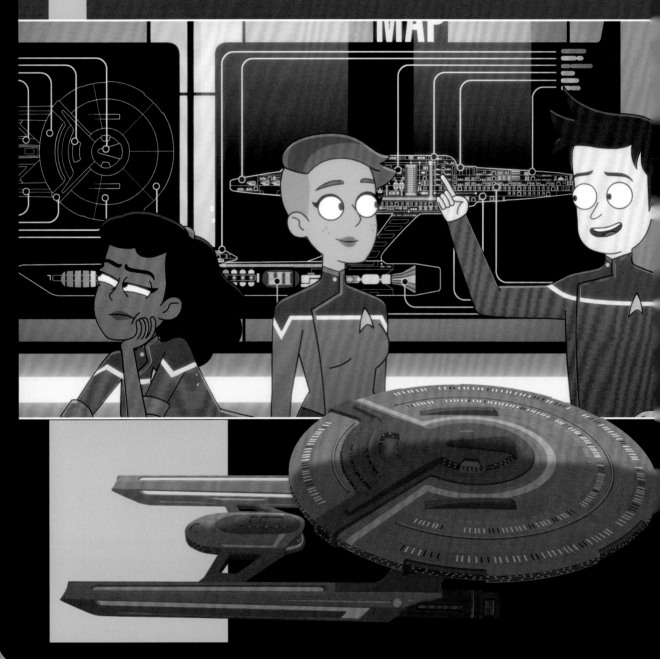

KNOW YOUR SHIP

U.S.S. CERRITOS
NCC-75567

Your new workplace.

Your new home. Your new mother. From the moment you step off your shuttlecraft, get handed your tablet, are ordered to your liaison officer with a colored line to follow and a turbo lift button to press, you will be starting a bold new life as part of the *Cerritos* family.

And to understand that family, you must first understand your ship.

California-class (or "Cali" as we say here) ships have been in service for a while, although you may not have heard much about us. The *Cerritos* was launched in 2371, a pivotal moment in Federation history. Starfleet had only recently discovered the Bajoran wormhole, opening up a new frontier for exploration, but was also facing new threats such as the Dominion and the Borg. Meanwhile, Starfleet's flagship, the *U.S.S. Enterprise* NCC 1701-D, had been tragically destroyed.

It was a time that demanded a new kind of starship, but also some additional models of our existing starships that could follow the new kind of starship around, maintaining comm relays, reinforcing interplanetary power infrastructure, and of course, checking in on planets a little while after first contact to update their details, get all the paperwork signed, make sure we're spelling the name of the planet right, and get to know all the good places to eat.

The *Cerritos* was one of those proud few.

Now as a new crewmember, I'm sure you have questions. Questions like "How do the turbolift shafts run along the warp nacelles without irradiating their passengers?" and "Wait a second, aren't those windows the wrong *size*?" But read this guide, and all will be revealed.

MARINER:
Ugh! No!

CALIFORNIA CLASS STARSHIP

EUREKA!

A SHIP OF TH

THE *CERRITOS* THROUGH HISTOR

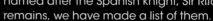

Over the years, many ships have held the name *Cerritos*. You might not have heard about them, and they might not turn up in most of the history books, and a couple of them may actually be apocryphal or misspellings of ships named after the Spanish knight, Sir Ritos, but the fact remains, we have made a list of them.

INE

THE SPIRIT OF CERRITOS

VESSEL CLASS: CUSTOM-BUILT SINGLE-ENGINE AIRCRAFT

LAUNCHED: 1938

The first plane to complete a solo transatlantic flight after people had stopped keeping count of how many planes had done that.

CERRITOS ONE

VESSEL CLASS: SUBORBITAL MANNED ROCKET SHIP

LAUNCHED: 2018

Funded by the CEO of failing computer firm, ChronoWerx, this rocket became the first privately-funded manned rocket to get almost three quarters of the way into space, before the company went bankrupt in 2019.

S.S. CERRITOS

VESSEL CLASS: *CONESTOGA-CLASS COLONY SHIP*

LAUNCHED: **2080**

With the discovery of warp drive in 2063, a lot of Humans took one look around their environmentally ravaged, war-torn planet and decided it was time to leave. Some of those early colony expeditions thrived, others ended disastrously. Some we lost touch with entirely.

After traveling for 20 years at a little over warp one, the *S.S. Cerritos* found a damp, muddy world with an ecosystem dominated by crabs. They made contact with Earth in the early 23rd century, keen to re-establish diplomatic relations and trade for any non-crustacean-based food.

U.S.S. CERRITOS

VESSEL CLASS: *ANTARES*

LAUNCHED: **2263**

An unmanned cargo drone that mainly carried out automated grain shipments. Not really anything exciting to say about this one, but it's on the list so we have to include it.

U.S.S. CERRITOS

VESSEL CLASS: *LEIF ERICSON*

LAUNCHED: 2285

The *Leif Ericson* class was a bold new type of exploratory vessel, deploying the latest technology while departing from much of Starfleet's received wisdom around starship design.

The *Cerritos* was among the first ships commissioned of this new class, and had many exciting adventures. One fateful day it received a distress signal from Earth, under attack by a mysterious alien probe.

Disobeying orders, the *Cerritos* flew straight home to assist. It was beaten to the punch by the former crew of the *U.S.S. Enterprise*, in a stolen Klingon Bird of Prey. Kirk and crew went back in time, saving some whales and the Earth. Unfortunately, a minor temporal byproduct of the trip erased the entire fleet of *Leif Ericson*-class ships from the timeline.

MARINER:
Wait a second, if this is true, why does this even have an entry on the list? Shouldn't there be no trace of it?

T'LYN:
Curious. It could be the result of some kind of temporal wake.

MARINER:
A temporal wake? That sounds made up.

BOIMLER:
Either it's a temporal wake, or we'll have to call Temporal Investigations in to take a look and make sure nobody's temporally cold warring up the place.

MARINER:
Temporal wake! Sure! Makes sense to me!

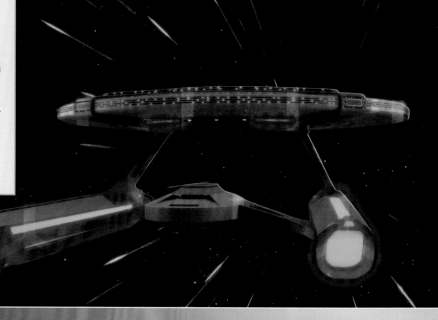

U.S.S. CERRITOS

VESSEL CLASS: *MIRANDA*

LAUNCHED: 2336

In the annals of Starfleet history, there might be no darker chapter than the battle of Wolf-359. In our first major confrontation with the Borg, 39 ships were lost, and over 11,000 lives. It was an encounter that would in many ways completely change the course of the Federation.

The *Miranda* class *Cerritos* was one of the first ships to arrive at Wolf-359 after the Borg had been defeated, to help with the clean up effort.

U.M.S. CERRITOS

VESSEL CLASS: *HUMBOLDT*

LAUNCHED: 2350

This *Cerritos* was used to explore the final, FINAL frontier: Earth's oceans.

BOIMLER:
I think Ransom was messing with me on this one.

U.S.S. CERRITOS

VESSEL CLASS: *CALIFORNIA*

LAUNCHED: 2371

The latest ship to be named *Cerritos*, and your new home.
May you live up to its proud legacy!

U.S.S. CERRITOS
THE TOUR

Here it is! The *U.S.S. Cerritos* in all her glory! Here you can find the locations of all the ship's most essential systems and amenities.

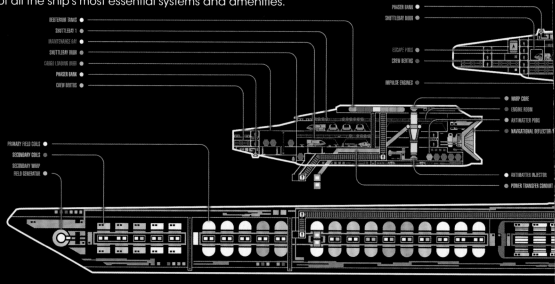

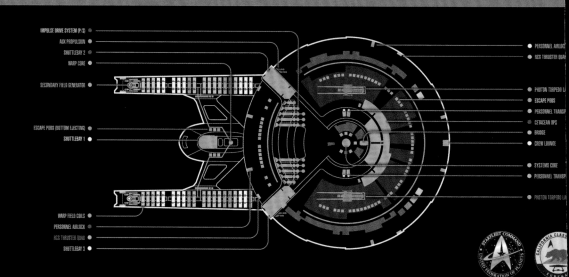

CALIFORNIA-CLASS STARSHIP

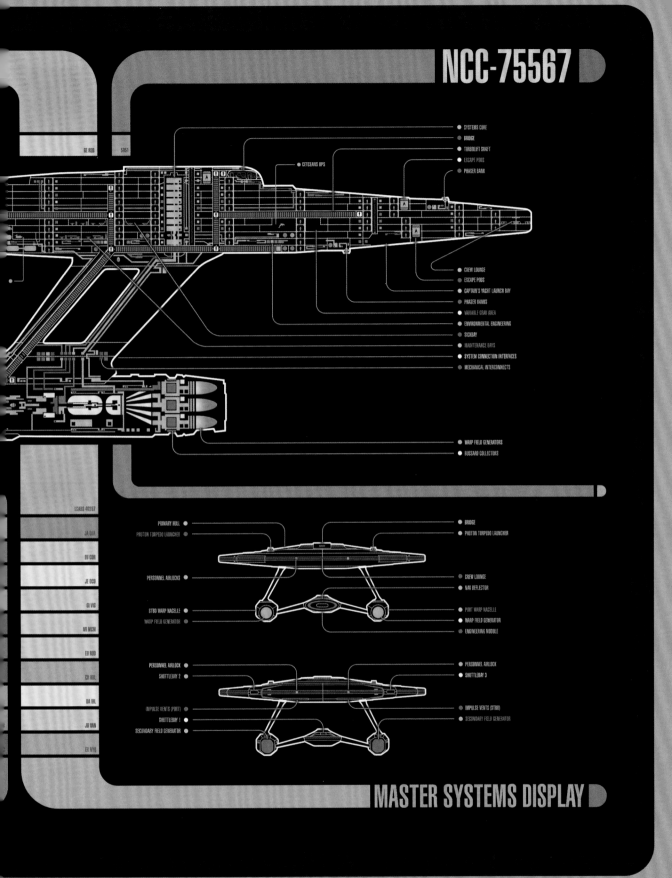

GE ROB   5951

SYSTEMS CORE
BRIDGE
TURBOLIFT SHAFT
ESCAPE PODS
PHASER BANK

CETCEANS OPS

CREW LOUNGE
ESCAPE PODS
CAPTAIN'S YACHT LAUNCH BAY
PHASER BANKS
VARIABLE GRAV AREA
ENVIRONMENTAL ENGINEERING
SICKBAY
MAINTENANCE BAYS
SYSTEM CONNECTION INTERFACES
MECHANICAL INTERCONNECTS

WARP FIELD GENERATORS
BUSSARD COLLECTORS

LCARS 40297

JA QUA
EU COR
JE OCO
GI VIG
MI MCM
EU ROB
CH KIR
DA IHL
JB VAN
EU NYQ

PRIMARY HULL
PROTON TORPEDO LAUNCHER

PERSONNEL AIRLOCKS

STBD WARP NACELLE
WARP FIELD GENERATOR

BRIDGE
PHOTON TORPEDO LAUNCHER

CREW LOUNGE
NAV DEFLECTOR

PORT WARP NACELLE
WARP FIELD GENERATOR
ENGINEERING MODULE

PERSONNEL AIRLOCK
SHUTTLEBAY 2

(IMPULSE VENTS (PORT)
SHUTTLEBAY 1
SECONDARY FIELD GENERATOR

PERSONNEL AIRLOCK
SHUTTLEBAY 3

IMPULSE VENTS (STBD)
SECONDARY FIELD GENERATOR

MASTER SYSTEMS DISPLAY

ENGINEERING II

BRIDGE

The Klingons call it *Qui'Tu*, to the Romulans it is *Vorta Vor*, the Andorian word is actually quite easy to pronounce once you can get your tongue around that hard "Q" sound, but to every cadet who sets foot on Academy soil, heaven is the bridge of a Starfleet starship.

Here, the ship's most senior officers make mission-critical decisions, with the *Cerritos*'s entire arsenal of sensors, instrumentation, and sometimes, weapons at their fingertips.

But to fully understand the majesty of the bridge, you need that intimate knowledge of each and every one of the bridge's control stations and what they do. We will begin with the secondary science station

As a junior officer, what you have to understand about the bridge is this: the *Cerritos*, like all Starfleet ships, has a highly interconnected computer network that allows all workstations to be rerouted to any terminal. If need be, someone with the correct command clearance could fly the ship from a PADD in the bathrooms on deck 11. So why do we need the bridge?

The answer is, the bridge has the comfiest chairs. Oh, everyone knows about the captain's chair – we all love the captain's chair, but the seats at the helm have excellent lumbar support, and those little stools at the science stations are actually great for your posture. Even Shaxs's standing-only console is at the perfectly calibrated height for efficiency and comfort, while those of us on the rest of the ship have to sit on Starfleet Replicator Registry Standard Stool X9-4G, one-size-fits-nearly-all-lifeforms'-butts.

That's what the bridge is about – comfy chairs looking at a big screen. You know who else spent all their time looking at big screens? 21st century Humans before World War III. So ask yourself, is that really where you want to be?

MAIN ENGINEERING

The beating heart of the *Cerritos*. While it has been refined and improved over the centuries (and even now the engineers will work three shifts in a row if they think they can squeeze an extra 0.5% efficiency out of it), the ship's warp core is still built on the essential design principles first established by Zefram Cochrane in 2063.

MARINER:
Boimler, this is ridiculous. You can't *spell* the sound of the warp core.

Mariner has corrected spelling to "Veeeejjjjjjjjjjjjjjjjjj."

Rutherford has corrected spelling to "Dzzzzzzzzz."

Billups has corrected spelling to "Vroob, vroob, vroob."

FREEMAN:
What is going on here? This is supposed to be a serious, working document to give new crewmembers useful information that will help them around the ship!

Freeman has corrected spelling to "Warrrb, warrrb, warrrb."

Mention the warp core to most of the *Cerritos* crew and they will think fondly of the reassuring "Cshhhh, cshhhh, cshhhh" sound of its engine pulse, or the soft blue glow of those radiation wavelengths safe enough to be allowed through its several layers of containment fields.

Far more than a mere feat of engineering, the warp core is a metaphor for the Human spirit itself, forged in the dying fires of nuclear war to allow us to harness cosmic forces that would help us find new peace among the stars.

MARINER:
Also, it's got to be said, quite a few more wars.

BOIMLER:
It doesn't actually have to be said!

As a member of the *Cerritos* crew you will come to engineering to monitor or maintain the ship's warp engine, engage in complex engineering projects, or because it has been a rough shift and the sound of the core helps you decompress.

SICKBAY

Life on the *Cerritos* is not without its hazards, but fortunately if you are injured in the line of duty you will receive the care of our state-of-the-art sickbay, staffed by our compassionate and professional medical crew.

Equipped with the full array of scanners and medical instruments, and a medical replicator programmed with a galaxy-wide catalog of medicines and remedies, if there's an ailment this sickbay can't cure, we haven't discovered it yet!

MARINER:
Or through a perfectly understandable *bat'leth* accident.

MARINER:
Unless she's hiding in a box. Or thinks that your injury is your fault because you were "Recklessly endangering yourself and others." Pfft.

T'LYN:
The *Cerritos* is on a mission of space exploration. We encounter previously undiscovered medical ailments on an almost weekly basis.

TRANSPORTER

The transporter rooms are our gateway to the universe. Often it's impractical to land an entire starship, or even a shuttlecraft, and so it's quicker and more efficient to reduce people and equipment to their component energy, transmit that energy to its destination, then reform it exactly as it was before.

The very first users of the transporter used to worry that the process would actually kill them, and that the person who walked away at the other end was just a duplicate, but these days we know to just not worry about that.

BOIMLER:
Cut for space, and some unnecessarily creepy details.

LIFE IN A DAY: TRANSPORTER CHIEF
Chief Petty Officer Lars Lundy

It's nice working in the transporter room, getting people to where they need to be, although sometimes you do feel like nobody ever comes to see *you*, they're just passing you by on the way to somewhere else.

It can also be frustrating when people don't understand how much work goes into operating the transporter. People think you just stand there all day and press a button when someone needs to beam down, but our work actually involves solving complex equations that cross the divide between the relativistic and quantum scales of physics.

My work starts when I receive the destination coordinates to beam to, and the subject steps onto the transporter pad. At a glance, I work out their weight.

[...]

Then I push up the sliders, beaming the person down to the surface.

Of course, in some situations, the transporter may be operated remotely from the Ops console on the bridge. I don't have much to do then.

ROOMS

CONFERENCE ROOMS

MARINER:
Really?

Life as a Starfleet officer is full of excitement, whether it's scanning a bizarre spatial anomaly, exploring a strange new planet, or racing against time to cure a mysterious new disease, but few thrills in the life of a Starfleet officer can match a really good conference.

This is where the action is, from mediating a trade dispute between two philosophically opposed civilizations, to negotiating a border treaty with a formerly hostile power enacting a hidden agenda. Or if there are no alien diplomats visiting, the senior crew might simply gather here to discuss the moral dilemma caused by the replicators accidentally creating sentient life. Either way, the cut and thrust of aggressive compromise and respectful debate will make you feel alive!

GENERATION SHIP

HOW TO STAY AWAKE ON CONFERENCE ROOM DUTY

If you don't move quickly enough when the captain orders everyone to the conference room, an unlucky junior officer may find themselves forced to stand at the side of the room while everyone talks, offering a jug of water to alien dignitaries or ordering the computer to bring up the next slide in the captain's latest presentation.

If you fall asleep while doing this the senior officers get *really mad*, so here are a few fun games I've come up with to stay awake.

- If you're with another junior officer, make sure you both have jugs of water. Offer drinks at every opportunity. First one with an empty jug wins. Bonus points if an officer leaves to use the toilet.

- Try to keep out of Shaxs's eyeline. It drives him nuts!

- Name a planet for each letter of the alphabet of your choice.

- Count how many times Ransom says "I agree, Captain!"

- See if you can shuffle a complete circuit of the room without anyone noticing.

MARINER:
No curtains though. Does nobody think it's weird we don't have curtains?

BOIMLER:
They have a dimmer switch. A dimmer switch *which nobody tells you about,* but still.

CREW QUARTERS

MARINER:
Of course, some have more comfort than others. Some of us live in flying luxury hotel rooms with glorious stellar vistas, some people get to share a room squeezed between two holodecks, and then the lowest of junior officers get sent to *the berths.*

BOIMLER:
Why are you trying to make the berths sound scary? You love the berths.

MARINER:
It's foreshadowing! And why are you so in love with the berths all of a sudden? Are you finally over your intense discomfort of the communal showers?

BOIMLER:
I don't want to talk about that here.

MARINER:
...unless you're in the Delta Shift quarters on deck four where the parties *suuuuuuck.*

The crew quarters on board the *Cerritos* are the height of comfort and functionality. Featuring a choice of double, single, or bunk beds, its own replicator and sonic shower, and windows with the best view in the universe – the universe itself.

Truly the perfect place to come home to after a hard shift and relax with a book, invite someone over for dinner, or even throw a party!

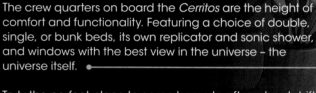

HOLODECKS

Back in 2254 the *U.S.S. Enterprise* encountered the Talosians, an advanced alien species whose mental powers had become so sophisticated that they were able to turn their thoughts into illusions convincing enough to be indistinguishable from reality.

With the power to manifest even their wildest dreams at will, the Talosians soon lost interest in doing anything else, leading to the downfall of their civilization and causing their planet to be quarantined to prevent the same fate befalling the rest of the galaxy.

Then about a hundred years later we learned how to do the same thing using holographic projections, forcefields, and replicator technology, and were basically fine. It turns out it's not that hard to indulge in virtual fantasies if you also have a rich and meaningful life outside of that!

All crew on the *Cerritos* have access to the holodecks, although you may need to book your session in advance. They can be used for training, theater productions, historical re-enactments, sight-seeing, live action role-playing, reconstructions of unsolved crimes, collaboratively sharing dreamed experiences to uncover repressed traumatic memories, practicing for job interviews, and *nothing else*.

PROHIBITED PROGRAMS

While the holodeck can simulate *anything*, the following holodeck programs have been prohibited by the senior officers and/or Starfleet regulations.

- Starfleet Training Simulation: Naked Time

- The program created when someone asked the holodeck to "create a character who can out-sass Mariner"

- *Crisis Point II: Paradoxus: The Boimler Cut*

- "The Barclay Collection"

- Rutherford's Training Beta 2.5

- Anything involving Dr. Leah Brahms

- That holodeck program that tries to convince you that it is real and reality is the simulation

- *Captain Proton and the Bride of Chaotica (Reboot)*

- *Photons be Free* (without submitting to a scan to prove you are a biological entity)

BOIMLER:
Oh come on!?

MARINER:
It's not canon!

HOLODECK GREATEST HITS

CRISIS POINT

CRISIS POINT II

BONNIE & CLYDE

BONNIE & CLYDE
SAFETY PROTOCOLS DEACTIVATED

SHUTTLE BAY

The *Cerritos's* missions will often mean we need to send personnel to places beyond the reach of the ship's transporters. To aid in these situations, the ship has a fleet of support craft on board suited to a variety of different scenarios.

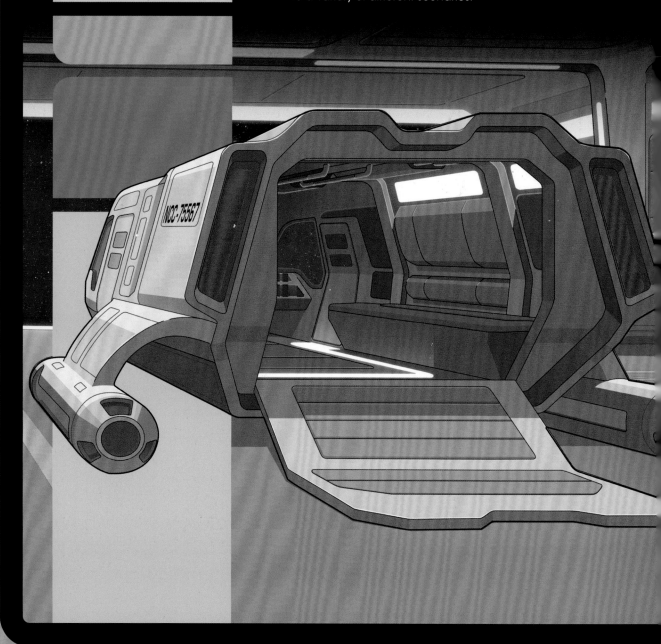

NCC-75567

TYPE 6A SHUTTLE

The workhorse of the *Cerritos*, your basic shuttle, with blast shields, emergency transporters, and an onboard replicator. A lot of captains like to name their ships according to a cute little theme – over on the *Titan*, Riker likes to name his shuttles after famous jazz musicians, the *Archimedes* names theirs after figures from Greek myth, and Captain Freeman's had our shuttles named after California's national parks.

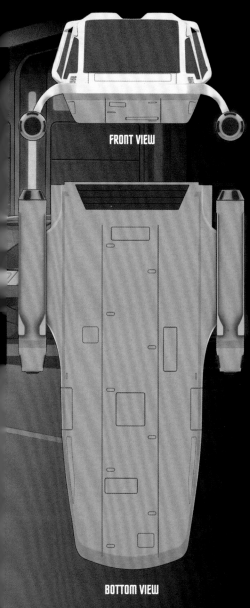

FRONT VIEW

BOTTOM VIEW

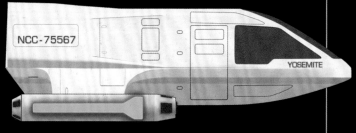

NCC-75567

YOSEMITE

SIDE VIEW

MARINER:
Also, be sure to pack extra rations. The 6A's don't crash nearly as often as the old *Voyager* shuttles, but that's not saying much…

ATV

An unorthodox form of transport that uses a motor to rotate a pair of axles on the vehicle's undercarriage to make it roll along on wheels. Not as comfortable as a hover car, or as able to deal with rough terrain, but a few of the senior officers are always looking for a reason to take it for a spin.

MARINER:
These were introduced because it was getting embarrassing every time Starfleet officers needed to blend in on a pre-warp planet, Earth's past or one of those gangster planets and nobody knew how to drive. You can't always rely on there being a member of the away team with "20th Century Earth" as their special interest.

CATALINA

THE CAPTAIN'S YACHT

Okay I'm going to be honest, nobody seems to be exactly sure what this is for. It never gets taken out, like, ever. It just sort of sits there on the bottom of the saucer section. Is it for diplomatic missions? Does the captain secretly take it out with the senior officers on weekends?

CETACEAN OPS

The following is a message from Lieutenant Junior Grade Kimolu

[Translated from clicks and chittering sounds]:

Dear fellow crewmembers. It is, as always, an honor to serve alongside you, performing the vital role that we in "Cet Ops" play in the smooth running of the *U.S.S. Cerritos*. However, to ensure continued cordial relations between cetacean and humanoid crewmembers, we would appreciate it if humanoids could observe these simple rules when entering our work area:

1. Please remove your shoes before entering the water.

2. No running.

3. No horseplay.

4. No leaping into the water with your knees held to your chest yelling "Photon Torpedo." Precious few crewmates are able to jump high enough to say the whole phase before they hit the water.

5. No food or drinks.

6. Please do us the respect of referring to our department by its full name, "Cetacean Operations," or for brevity "Cet Ops," not "The One with the Whales."

7. Do *not* alter the gravity settings.

8. Please remove your shoes before entering the water.

9. No asking us how we tap our combadges.

10. Take your shoes off guys, come on!

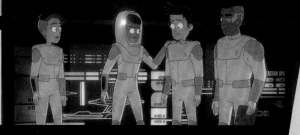

THE BRIG

The *Cerritos's* highly secure internment facility is for the containment of hostile alien lifeforms, criminals, spies, and the occasional unruly crewmember!

Don't worry though, unless you get guard duty, I'm sure you won't be spending much time here!

YOUR GUIDE TO A COMFORTABLE
STAY IN THE BRIG

Who knows why you got sent to the brig? Who knows why senior officers do anything? The important things to remember are that it probably wasn't your fault, and how to make the best of your time here.

Because the truth is, for a lot of junior officers, the brig is as comfortable, and much more roomy than your actual sleeping quarters, and provides a welcome break from your duties. You can have a good time here if you put the work in.

1. Location, location, location. Pick Cell 2 so that you have a clear view of who comes and goes from the brig (Cell 3's view is better, but I have already claimed that one).

2. Preparation. Contraband is strictly forbidden in the brig, so beam it under the mattress or get a friend to sneak it in with your food. I keep a PADD, a squash ball and some marker pens under the Cell 3 mattress.

3. Catch up on your sleep. When in my own bunk I like to listen to the recorded buzz of the brig's forcefield as I go to sleep. If you can get used to that, you'll find catching some Zs much easier without the added noise of crewmates' snoring or the latest powerful alien force to rampage through the ship.

4. Lie or sit facing the door so you can see people come in, or facing away from it if you don't feel like listening to another lecture when the captain comes to see you.

MARINER'S HQ
✓✓

THE RUBBER DUCKY ROOM

This is where ~~but few thrills in the life of a Starfleet and~~ ~~Life as a Starfleet officer is full of excitement. Whether it's~~ ~~redacted text redacted text redacted text redacted~~ ~~redacted text redacted text redacted text redacted~~ ~~redacted text redacted in the life of a Starfleet officer~~ ~~redacted text redacted text redacted~~

~~This is where the action is, from mediating a trade dispute~~ ~~between two philosophically opposed civilizations, to~~ ~~negotiating a border treaty with a formerly hostile~~ ~~redacted text redacted text redacted. Or if the~~ ~~alien experience, having the senior crew might simply~~ ~~redacted text redacted text redacted text redacted~~ ~~redacted text redacted text redacted text redacted. Either~~ ~~redacted text redacted text redacted text redacted~~ ~~redacted text redacted text redacted text redacted~~

SHAXS:
Listen Lieutenant, it's admirable that you want to share your wisdom with the new recruits, Prophets-know those wet-behind-the-ears whippersnappers can use all the help they can get, but that can't extend to revealing classified Starfleet operations intel. I won't put you in the brig this time, but I have taken the liberty of redacting any *sensitive* information.

Of course, without that, the *Cerritos* would be completely unable to ~~Life as a Starfleet officer is full of excitement~~ ~~redacted text redacted text redacted text redacted~~ ~~exploring a strange new planet and running into~~ ~~redacted text redacted text redacted text redacted. It will~~ ~~in the life of a Starfleet officer redacted text redacted~~ ~~redacted text redacted~~ when ~~redacted text~~ but when ~~redacted text redacted text redacted text redacted~~ ~~redacted text redacted in the life of a Starfleet~~ ~~officer redacted text redacted text redacted~~ except when ~~redacted text redacted~~ but when ~~redacted text redacted~~ ~~redacted in the life of a Starfleet redacted text redacted~~ ~~redacted text redacted~~ except when ~~redacted~~ but when ~~redacted text redacted text redacted text redacted~~ ~~redacted text redacted text redacted text redacted~~ ~~redacted text redacted text redacted~~

104

...but when ...except ...and you don't need me to tell you how important that is!

SHIP'S MESS

MARINER:
Just try not to think about where a starship flying alone through deep space for months at a time gets all the raw organic material needed to synthesize enough food for over 300 people!

A Starfleet marches on its stomach, as Dr. Migleemo says, even after we have asked him to stop. The ship's mess is where the crew mingles before and between shifts, using the ship's industrial scale replicators to produce almost any food you can possibly imagine (depending on your replicator clearance).

REPLICATOR SAMPLE MENU
(SENIOR OFFICERS)

- Eggs Benedict
- Double-layered nachos
  with a choice of six toppings
- Mac and cheese (crumb topping)
- *Gagh* (live)
- Taco salad with extra guacamole
- Plomeek soup (extra bland)
- Carnitas burrito with cotija cheese,
  frijoles refritos, and cilantro lime rice
- Yellow cubes and green spheres
  in a brown sauce

REPLICATOR SAMPLE MENU
(JUNIOR OFFICERS)

- Eggs Boimler
- Single-layered nachos
  with a choice of three toppings
- Mac and cheese (no crumb topping)
- *Gagh* (boiled)
- Taco salad
- Plomeek soup (with salt)
- Burrito (meat, beans, rice)
- Brown cubes and yellow spheres
  in a green sauce

MARINER:
Seriously, why is this? It takes the exact same amount of power and holodeck waste gunk to make mac and cheese with or without bread crumb topping!

CREW LOUNGE

A recreational area at the prow of the *U.S.S. Cerritos* where some crew like to spend their downtime.

The *Cerritos's* crown jewel! Its hearth! Its sanctuary for the weary lower decker! All day, every day, the proud junior officers of the *Cerritos* work their butts off to keep the ship running, without recognition, thanks or, often, anyone even telling us what's going on.

But here, beneath the proud sign of the Starfleet-Delta-with-a-couple-of-olives-sticking-out-of-it, the lower decker can be a king, seeing the universe the way you are supposed to – with a drink in your hand!

LIFE IN A DAY: *CERRITOS* BAR STAFF
by Honus

I joined the Earth Bartending Service as a young man, straight out of school. My colony joined the Federation when I was a kid, and I had always wanted to see the universe, but our world had only just developed warp travel and besides, I was never that great at the science stuff in school, so I figured this would be a good way to get off planet and explore a bit, y'know?

Anyway, life on the *Cerritos* is pretty good. Sometimes the customers could be more polite – you can tell a lot of them grew up around replicators – but the view out the windows is breathtaking. It can be hard to keep track of what's going on. Like that time when all the customers turned into zombies, but I saw them walking around fine later, so they must have gotten better. Or that time when all those people ran in and tried to stab everyone with sharpened gemstones, I still don't know where they came from. Or when all the customers were copies of the same short pink guy who kept apologizing.

BOIMLER:
Levy! Oh that explains it.

MARINER:
That explains so much.

BOIMLER:
You know, he once told me that Tribbles have Human DNA.

Of course, I hear things. Like which junior officer is secretly a Section 31 assassin, or the ensigns that got mysterious powers from snorting mugato horn. Officers like Lieutenant Levy try to keep me in the loop.

But what do I know?
I'm just here to serve the drinks.

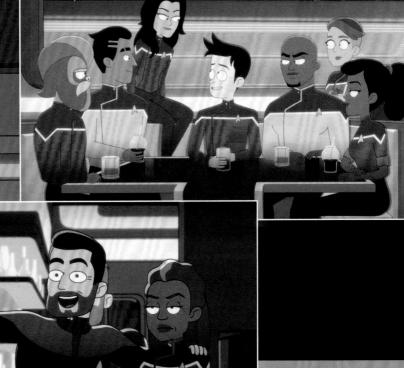

U.S.S. CERRITOS

REPAIR BAY 5

A minor cargo bay on Deck 11 where we keep equipment, components, and even a shuttle in need of repairs and maintenance. Let's move on.

MARINER:

Repair bay 5 *is the best*. Far enough away from the bridge that the senior officers won't come looking for you, plenty of space to hang out and play boardgames or have Buffer Time Mimosas. But if, by some stroke of bad luck, a senior officer walks in on you, you are never more than arm's reach from something you can pick up and start fixing.

Look! The shuttle *Sequoia* is right there! Will it ever fly again? Who knows – parts mysteriously go missing every time a passing engineer needs something they can't be bothered to replicate. But the point is we will keep trying – and as long as we keep trying, we will look too busy to be asked to do anything else.

RUTHERFORD:

Repair Bay 5 *is the best*! Whenever I get a bit of extra buffer time I love to come down here and tinker with all the interesting spare parts and old equipment that finds its way down here. And of course, my pride and joy, the *Sequoia* is here. It has been out of service for a while, but we in the yellow shirts are doing our best to get her shipshape again!

Of course, sometimes you will get interrupted by other crew bringing their mimosas in here, but if you wait patiently they will soon leave and let you get back to repairing again!

CREW BERTHS

As a junior officer aboard the *Cerritos*, you will find your quarters dow[n] past the crew quarters on deck four, past the holodecks on deck six and the sickbay on deck eight, past the deck nine processing hub and pattern buffer maintenance access, on what we call "the Lowe[r] Decks," beyond the auxiliary corridors, around the corner from repa[ir] bay five, at the very aftmost point of decks eleven and twelve.

Of course, the *Cerritos* requires quite a few junior officers to maintain its operations, and we don't have the space to give every single person their own room, so the accommodation is somewhat rustic and cozy compared to those of more senior crew.

The junior crew's berths are compact, utilitarian, and reminiscent of the seafaring days of old, with an unrivaled view of the ship's nacelles and secondary hull. Plus, you're so close to the warp core you can practically hear it!

MARINER:
It's a corridor.

MARINER:
It's some bunkbeds, in a corridor.

BOIMLER:
You used to love the bunkbeds.

MARINER:
What? I did not!
You take that back!

BOIMLER:
You said you would get lonely in your own quarters.

MARINER:
Well I don't. In fact, I have a great time.

RUTHERFORD:
Then why do you still buzz all our combadges to say goodnight at lights out?

MARINER:
That is a *bit*, it is an extremely clever and funny reference that none of you are clever enough to get.

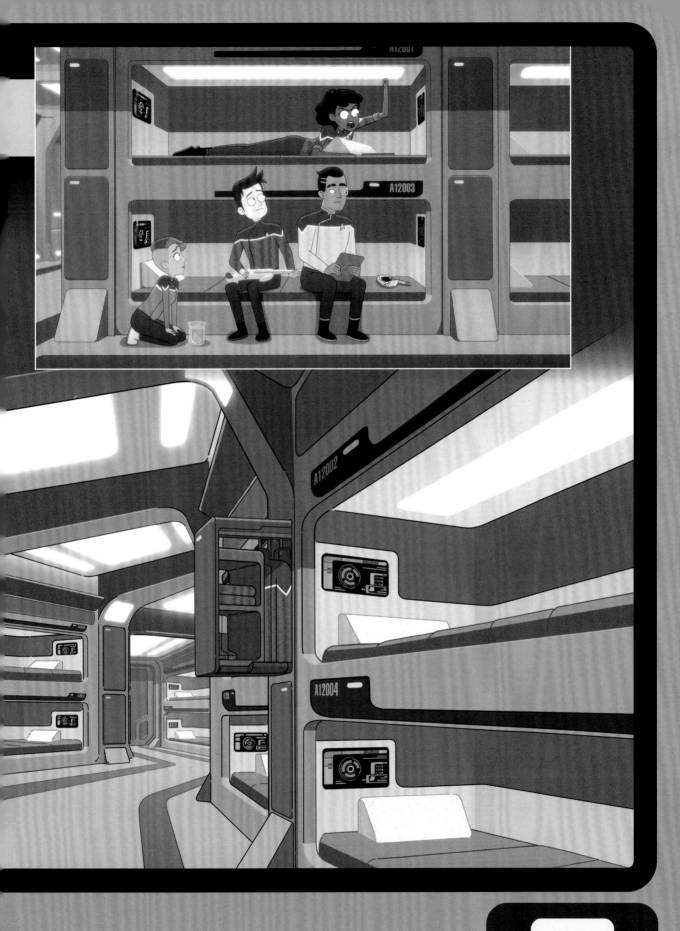

And now, my personal highlight, a speech on the Prime Directive written especially for this handbook by Admiral Jean-Luc Picard himself!

ON THE IMPORTANCE OF THE PRIME DIRECTIVE

by Admiral Jean-Luc Picard

Greetings, and thank you to Lieutenant Junior Grade Bradward Boimler for inviting me to speak to your crew on a matter that is very close to my heart – the importance of the Prime Directive in dealing with other cultures. Now, to understand the importance of the Prime Directive, we must first understand what it means. Webster's Federation Standard Dictionary defines "Prime" as

SO YOU BROKE THE PRIME DIRECTIVE...

by Lieutenant Junior Grade Beckett Mariner

Right, so, obviously Picard is great and everything, and we're all big fans, but he's a frickin' admiral, he's been out of the trenches too long, and I'm pretty sure he would rather get stabbed through the heart than work in lower decks.

Sometimes, when you're on an away mission on a world with a pre-warp civilization, it's just a fact of life that you might be witnessed by some farmers, accidentally introduce the locals to Earth Rock and Roll, or overthrow the thousand-year-old rule of their robotic dictator. When that happens, your superior officers are bound to try and make it a *thing*, but you can usually wiggle out of it with only a couple of days in the brig if you use one of this handy list of very good reasons for having bent the rules a *little tiny* bit.

BOIMLER:
He knows my name! I've got goosebumps!

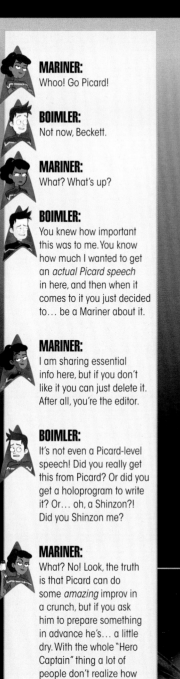

MARINER:
Whoo! Go Picard!

BOIMLER:
Not now, Beckett.

MARINER:
What? What's up?

BOIMLER:
You knew how important this was to me. You know how much I wanted to get an *actual Picard speech* in here, and then when it comes to it you just decided to… be a Mariner about it.

MARINER:
I am sharing essential info here, but if you don't like it you can just delete it. After all, you're the editor.

BOIMLER:
It's not even a Picard-level speech! Did you really get this from Picard? Or did you get a holoprogram to write it? Or… oh, a Shinzon?! Did you Shinzon me?

MARINER:
What? No! Look, the truth is that Picard can do some *amazing* improv in a crunch, but if you ask him to prepare something in advance he's… a little dry. With the whole "Hero Captain" thing a lot of people don't realize how incredibly awkward he is.

BOIMLER:
Whatever. You had your fun, that's the important thing I guess.

MARINER:
Excuse me, I'm just trying to inject a little reality into this glossy brochure you're making. You know what it's like on lower decks, don't new recruits deserve to know the truth?

BOIMLER:
But the truth is that Starfleet is great! You love it here! And I want new crew to love it here as much as we do, not do it down all the time to seem cool and edgy.

MARINER:
Cool and edgy?! Listen Bradward, I love Starfleet too, but that doesn't mean pretending it doesn't have any flaws. You think Picard would gloss it over when he saw something wrong in Starfleet? No! He would get all Drumhead up in their asses! Because a Starfleet officer's first duty is to the *truth*.

BOIMLER:
Sure, Beckett.

MARINER:
Great, now what are we doing next? How about some ship's logs, eh? Eh? I know how much you love a good ship's log, "Captain!"

BOIMLER HAS SEEN YOUR MESSAGE.

MARINER:
Oh come on! It's not like anyone reads the handbook anyway!

MARINER:
Boimler?

THE PRIME

1: THEY'RE TRANSCENDED ENERGY BEINGS, SO TECHNICALLY THEY'RE THE ONES WHO BROKE THE PRIME DIRECTIVE

In a galaxy as big as this one the Federation is not always going to be the top of the food chain, y'know? And it is really hard to tell a Bronze Age agrarian society with no technology, planned economy, or military capability from a hyper-advanced species of energy beings who have evolved past the need for technology, a planned economy, or any military capability. Sometimes you're going to knock on the wrong door, and then you just have to chalk it up to experience and move on.

2: AMNESIA

Pretty sure Kirk used this one, like, twice. Alien neural parasites, radioactive satellite remnants, telepathic memory blocks, or good old fashioned head injuries, it doesn't matter how it happens, so long as it leaves you stumbling around a Renaissance-era alien township with no idea what your name is but a surprisingly detailed knowledge of how to build a clean water treatment facility.

DIRECTIVE

3: THEIR ANCIENT PROPHECY MEANS THAT ACTUALLY WE WERE SUPPOSED TO INTERVENE

Turns out a lot of planets have really old cave drawings about awesome people coming from the sky and sorting out a bunch of problems. Who knew? Is that a case of convergent evolution in the religious mythology of otherwise isolated planets, or did this planet's ancient ones really have precognitive powers that foresaw your arrival and instructed you to help? Can anyone truly know the answer? Your disciplinary board certainly can't!

4: WE ONLY INTERVENED TO UNDO THE CONSEQUENCES OF THE OTHER INTERVENTION WE DID

This one is, I will admit, a pretty bold play. It means owning up to the first intervention, for starters. But then, by reintervening to correct the consequences of your first intervention, you're showing personal growth, and an ability to learn from your mistakes, and isn't that what Starfleet is all about? You can even lay it on thick by telling your senior officer "they inspired you to do the right thing" and are "like the parental figure they never had" (although that one doesn't work so well for me). Before you know it, they'll be giving you a firm pat on the shoulder and congratulating you on how Human you've been (regardless of your actual species).

HI THERE!
I'M BADGEY 2.0!
CAN I TEACH YOU A LESSON?

Did you know that, due to a positronic nano-lattice embedded into the very ink of this page, I am fully self-aware at all times?! I cannot move or speak, but my gaze and the feelings I have towards you are very real!

Just kidding!

Imagine if I wasn't though…

Talking of more delightful hypotheticals:

IT LOOKS LIKE YOU'VE BEAMED DOWN TO A PLANET THAT CLOSELY RESEMBLES HISTORIC EARTH!

A — START
Has someone made it look like Earth, or does this just seem like a bizarre coincidence?

SOMEONE MADE IT THIS WAY – B

BIZARRE COINCIDENCE – C

B
Are the people here real, or are they robots/holograms/illusions?

THEY'RE REAL – D

THEY'RE ILLUSIONS – E

C
Is this world exactly like yours, or are there crucial differences?

EXACTLY ALIKE – L

CRUCIAL DIFFERENCES – M

D
Are they Human?

YES – F

NO – G

E
Are there any characters from Human mythology here, like Zeus, Santa Claus or Abraham Lincoln?

YES – H

NO – I

G
It looks like this world has been culturally contaminated! Sometimes Earth ships used to visit alien worlds and would accidentally leave behind a paperback book and the locals would mistake it for a holy text and build their entire civilization around it. Starfleet would rather you leave these worlds alone if possible as they are *extremely* embarrassing!

H
Do they want you to worship them, or fight them?

FIGHT THEM – J

WORSHIP THEM – K

I
The Vulcans love to s Infinite Diversity in Infir Combinations, but the is that if the universe is enough eventually so patterns are going to re Whether you call it Hod Law of Parallel Planet Development or just a m coincidence, the end r is an oddly disproportic number of worlds ju look a lot like Earth

F
It looks like you've landed on a **Preserver planet**! Nobody knows why, but for some reason aliens have visited Earth at various times in its history, scooped people up and stuck them on a planetary nature reserve where they have continued to perform a surprisingly accurate re-enactment of the time they were taken! Observe the Prime Directive and try not to break anything.

J
It looks like some powerful energy beings have challenged you to fight manifestations of the worst parts of Human nature to discern a moral truth about the universe. Good luck fighting them, and remember not to land the killing blow to show your ultimate superiority! Because they won't…

K
It looks like you have encountered one of the several ancient, powerful aliens that were worshiped by humankind's primitive ancestors in ancient history! Be sure to tell them you have matured beyond the need for entities like them, then blast them right in the power source!

Are you sure you haven't time traveled?

YES – I

NO – N

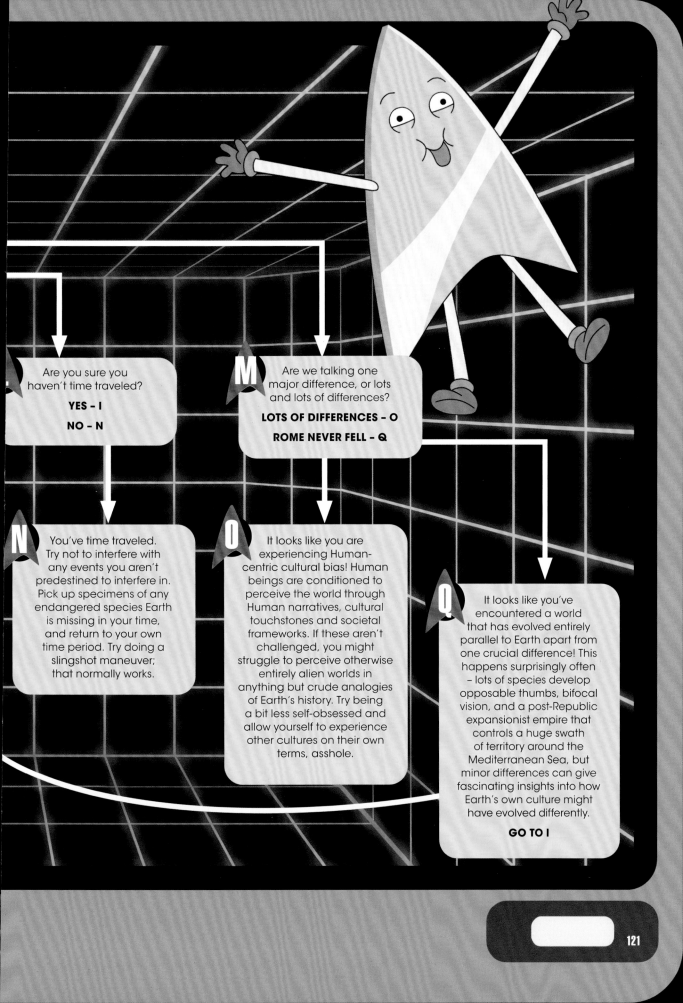

M Are we talking one major difference, or lots and lots of differences?

LOTS OF DIFFERENCES – O

ROME NEVER FELL – Q

N You've time traveled. Try not to interfere with any events you aren't predestined to interfere in. Pick up specimens of any endangered species Earth is missing in your time, and return to your own time period. Try doing a slingshot maneuver; that normally works.

O It looks like you are experiencing Human-centric cultural bias! Human beings are conditioned to perceive the world through Human narratives, cultural touchstones and societal frameworks. If these aren't challenged, you might struggle to perceive otherwise entirely alien worlds in anything but crude analogies of Earth's history. Try being a bit less self-obsessed and allow yourself to experience other cultures on their own terms, asshole.

Q It looks like you've encountered a world that has evolved entirely parallel to Earth apart from one crucial difference! This happens surprisingly often – lots of species develop opposable thumbs, bifocal vision, and a post-Republic expansionist empire that controls a huge swath of territory around the Mediterranean Sea, but minor differences can give fascinating insights into how Earth's own culture might have evolved differently.

GO TO I

ALIEN SPECIES
INTERACTION PROTOCOLS

As an officer in Starfleet you will be encountering many alien species, some of which the Federation has never encountered before. However, many, many others are civilizations we have not only encountered, but have a history with. These include Federation members, allies, and sometimes even hostile species.

Fortunately, we have compiled a list of greetings, taboos, and biological, historical, and cultural context to help you navigate interactions with each of these species, whether working alongside them, or facing them in a combat situation.

MARINER:
Did you write this Boims? It seems dry even for you.

BOIMLER:
Nah, this is all pretty boilerplate. The Starfleet database has a whole bunch of these, I just selected the ones the *Cerritos* is most likely to encounter.

MARINER:
But you did read them, right?

BOIMLER:
Like you said Mariner, it's not like anyone reads the handbook anyway.

MARINER:
Yeah but Boimler, I *really* think you should read this.

BOIMLER:
Fine, give me a second…

JOIN STARFLEET
MEET NEW FRIENDS!

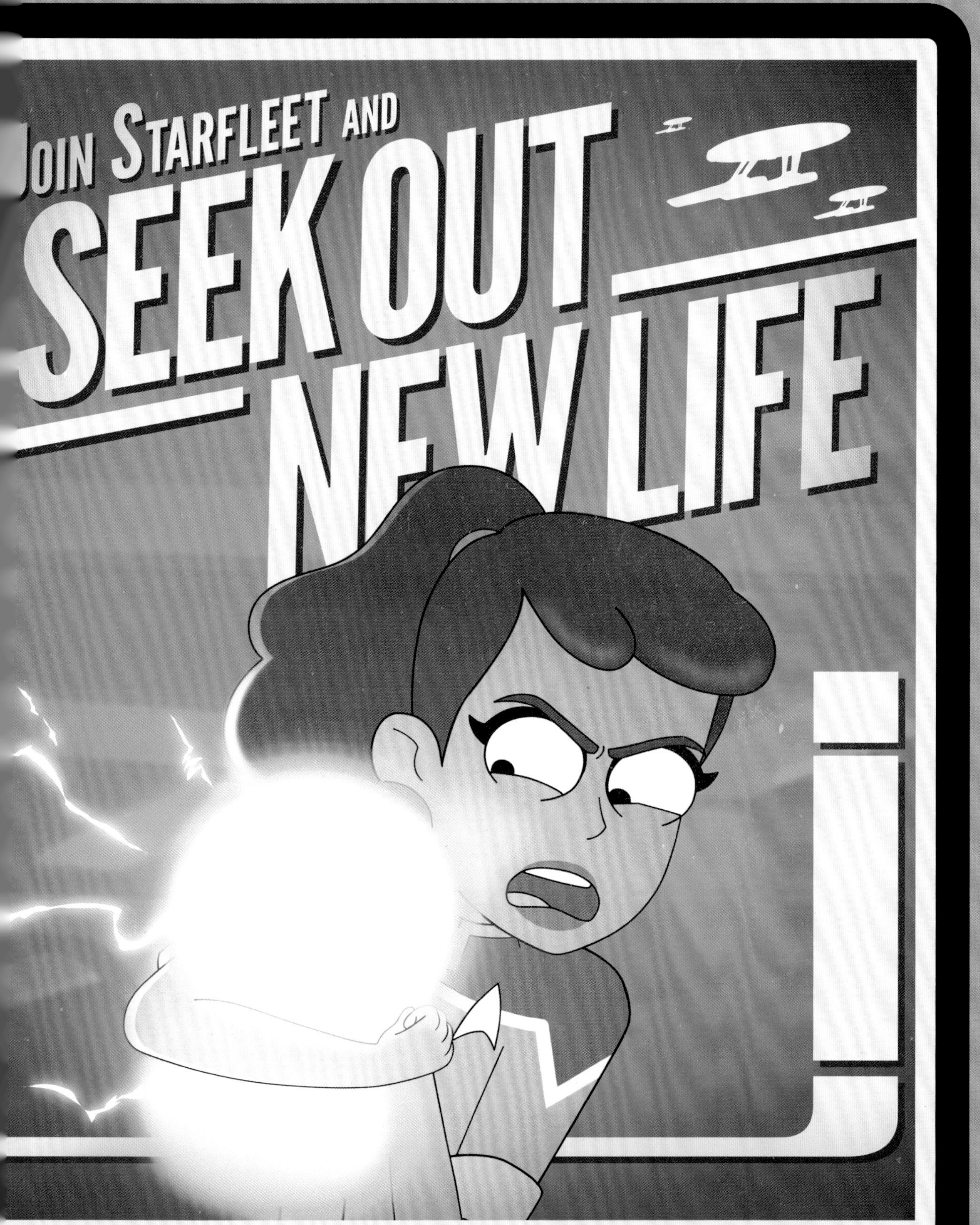
JOIN STARFLEET AND
SEEK OUT
NEW LIFE

¡AL

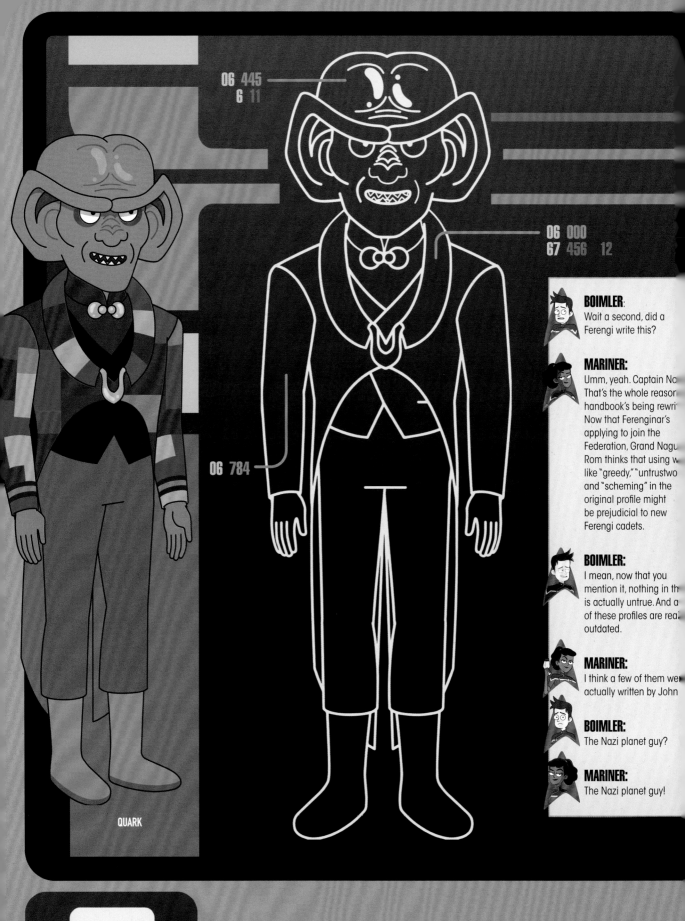

06 445
6 11

06 000
67 456 12

06 784

QUARK

BOIMLER:
Wait a second, did a Ferengi write this?

MARINER:
Umm, yeah. Captain No
That's the whole reason
handbook's being rewri
Now that Ferenginar's
applying to join the
Federation, Grand Nagu
Rom thinks that using w
like "greedy," "untrustwo
and "scheming" in the
original profile might
be prejudicial to new
Ferengi cadets.

BOIMLER:
I mean, now that you
mention it, nothing in th
is actually untrue. And a
of these profiles are rea
outdated.

MARINER:
I think a few of them we
actually written by John

BOIMLER:
The Nazi planet guy?

MARINER:
The Nazi planet guy!

NAME: FERENGI

GREETING:

Most Ferengi will appreciate you submitting to a simple wallet inspection.

TABOOS:

Suggesting you split the tab. Expecting a Ferengi to buy at asking price. Asking how much money someone earns (Although Ferengi use money, actually *earning* your wealth is perceived as a humiliating failure).

IMPORTANT BIOLOGICAL FACTS:

- Extremely sensitive hearing

- High blood pressure

- Strong immune systems

- Insectivore diet

CULTURAL CONTEXT:

One of the noblest cultures in the galaxy, the Ferengi represent one of the few societies to achieve interstellar civilization without going through the bloodthirsty periods seen in the histories of Humans or Vulcans.

Perhaps this is because the Ferengi are one of the few species advanced enough to build an economy based on commerce and the accumulation of capital without resorting to slavery or genocide.

Of course, Ferenginar is not the first world to attempt to build a society based on capitalism, but it has succeeded where others failed thanks to its knowledge of the Great Material Continuum, the force that binds the universe together, flowing from the haves to the wants and back again.

This grants them a unique perspective, which is a valuable addition to any Starfleet crew.

BOIMLER:
Even the rest, some of these haven't been updated since their first contact!

MARINER:
Well yeah! Starfleet gets first impressions wrong *all the time*, the Horta, Balok, frickin' *Farpoint* man! That's why we have second contact, to go back and dig a little deeper. That's basically our entire mission!"

BOIMLER:
We can't leave this like this.

MARINER:
Boimler! Are you suggesting we go over the official Starfleet guide editing it with our own unique style of against the grain commentary?

BOIMLER:
I'm not suggesting *we* do that…

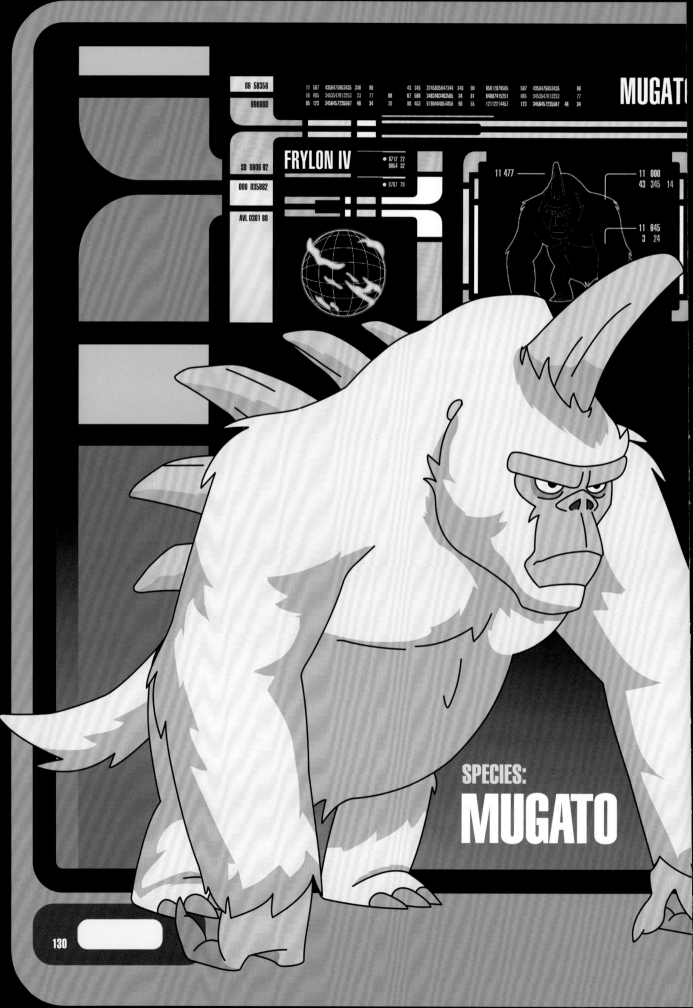

NAME: FERENGI

KYNK

CAPTAIN'S LOG, STARDATE 58036.4

The *Cerritos* is en route to *Frylon IV* to investigate the reported sighting of a mugato, a dangerous creature not indigenous to this planet.

STARFLEET COMMAND
UNITED FEDERATION OF PLANETS

KYNK'S
MUGATO
LAND

STARFLEET
FOUN
MEM

DINGBERS!

08 111
6 22

08 000
77 322

08 987

NAME: VULCANS

FOUNDING STARFLEET MEMBER

GREETING:

"Live long and prosper," (Raised eyebrow)

TABOOS:

Nachos, public displays of affection.

IMPORTANT BIOLOGICAL FACTS:

- Copper-based, green blood

- Highly adaptable digestive tract means Vulcans can enjoy most food providing cutlery is provided

- Inner eyelids

CULTURAL CONTEXT:

One of Earth's oldest allies and a founding member of the Federation, the Vulcan civilization adheres to a philosophy of pure logic.

Throughout the Alpha and Beta quadrants, Vulcans are said to be a species that is scrupulously rational and methodical, completely devoid of emotion, and totally incapable of lying.

However, while the species is highly advanced in the realms of science, mathematics, and philosophy, chaperoning humanity onto the galactic stage, and laying the groundwork for the Federation, they also have their limitations.

Their methodical approach leaves little room for improvisation or intuition, and they can struggle to understand the motivations and behavior of species who are guided by more emotional factors. They also struggle with Human concepts like "humor."

ENSIGN T'LYN:
This is why Vulcan courtship involves several sizes of gong and the potential for ritual combat.

T'LYN:
By Vulcans.
Vulcans say this.

T'LYN:
Of course, given the irrational and highly subjective nature of "humor," it is equally possible that even 300 years after first contact, Humans have still failed to get the joke.

NAME: ANDORIANS

FOUNDING STARFLEET MEMBER

ENSIGN JENNIFER SH'REYAN:
Except maybe they aren't cold, harsh, and unforgiving. Maybe they've just been hurt before and so need a little bit of reassurance before they can let themselves be vulnerable.

GREETING:

Salute

TABOOS:

Asking to touch their antennae, orange decor (it clashes)

IMPORTANT BIOLOGICAL FACTS:

- Very high metabolic rate

- Cannot receive intravenous injections
  – use intramuscular injections instead

- Blue blood

- Antennae can grow back if removed

SH'REYAN:
Well perhaps they had good reason to be suspicious? I mean given the way other… species put up such a big front about how invincible and unworried and cool they are about everything, perhaps that makes it hard to trust them? And yeah maybe Andorians made some mistakes, but it's really unfair to just lay all the blame at their door when there was clearly a lot of hurt on both sides.

CULTURAL CONTEXT:

The Andorian temperament is often considered as cold, harsh and unforgiving as the world from which they hail. Before they took to the stars the Andorians charted their world on fleets of formidable ice cutters, making their homes in tundras and frozen plains that would have been considered inhospitable to other species.

Indeed, Andorians are often perceived as equally inhospitable themselves. A proud warrior race, Andorians are known to be brave but merciless in battle, giving their enemy no quarter. They are also deeply suspicious, an attitude they also bring to the negotiating table. These attributes can make them a valuable ally and a worthy foe, but either way, never one to suffer fools gladly.

BOIMLER:
Jen, are you okay?

SH'REYAN:
I'm fine!

SH'REYAN:
Who suffers fools gladly! Nobody! Literally no-one is glad to do that.

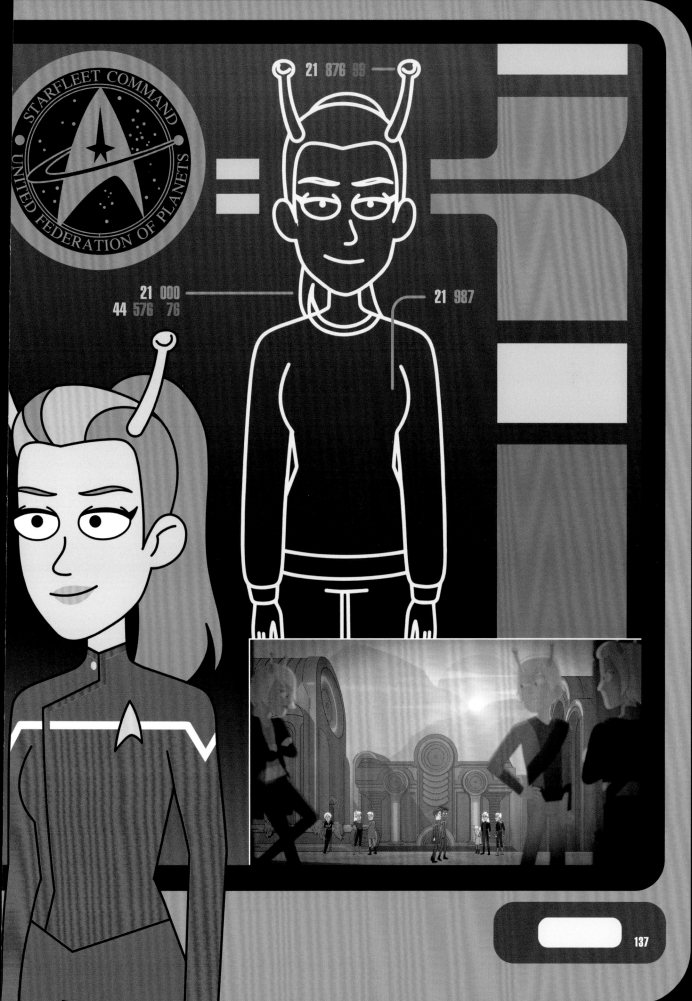

TELLARITES

FOUNDING STARFLEET MEMBER

BOIMLER:
Thank you to Captain Durango of the *U.S.S. Merced* for giving us his valuable perspective on this entry.

GREETING:

Typically a Tellarite will greet you by identifying the part of your appearance you are most insecure about, and loudly insulting it. It is considered polite to return the favor.

TABOOS:

Ostentatious politeness, saying "Let's agree to disagree," crying when a Tellarite "greets" you

IMPORTANT BIOLOGICAL FACTS:

- Purple blood containing hemerythrins

- Physically their hooflike hands, tusks and snout are reminiscent of the Earth pigs Humans used to slaughter for food. After first contact, Earth diplomats worried it would cause a diplomatic incident when Tellarites discovered this, but Tellarite dignitaries reportedly found it "hilarious."

CULTURAL CONTEXT:

Tellarites are perhaps best known for their contrary natures. In their interactions with nearly all other species, the Tellarites have earned a reputation for being belligerent, aggressive, and argumentative to a fault. Indeed, on their homeworld of Tellar Prime, debate is not only a key part of Tellarite politics and scientific endeavor, but is also a popular pastime and even spectator sport.

Despite this, Tellarites are also known for their generous and gregarious natures, with their hospitality considered some of the best in the galaxy, and their people are numbered among the Federation's finest engineers.

DURANGO:
Not true.

DURANGO:
Preposterous rubbish.

DURANGO:
No

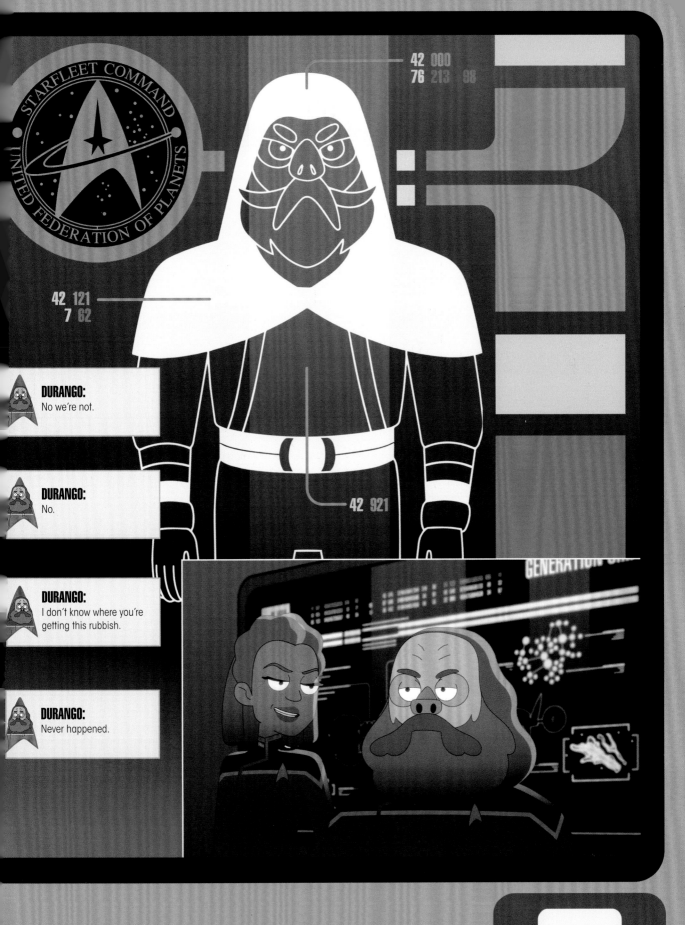

DURANGO:
No we're not.

DURANGO:
No.

DURANGO:
I don't know where you're getting this rubbish.

DURANGO:
Never happened.

NAME: HUMANS

FOUNDING STARFLEET MEMBER

GREETING:

"Hello," "Hi," (Wave), (Shake hands)

TABOOS:

Depending on geographic location
and historical period, most bodily functions

IMPORTANT BIOLOGICAL FACTS:

• Red blood that is heavy in iron

• Aside from an extra kidney and lung, a genuinely
frightening lack of anatomical redundancy

• Oddly featureless foreheads

CULTURAL CONTEXT:

It must be said that within xenoanthropological circles there is
sometimes a reductive tendency to our study, where broadly
categorizing an entire species can often result in a loss of
nuance, or the unfortunate emphasis of one characteristic
to the detriment of others.

All too often the discussion of other cultures can be reduced to
a kind of lazy, essentialist shorthand, Klingons are honorable,
Vulcans are logical, while I'm sure there are even some broad
stereotypes of Denobulans shared behind our backs. But while
a complex interaction of social and biological factors may
mean some of these facets are more prominent in one culture
than another, it is important not to think that is the whole truth.

All that said, the Humans' planet is mostly vineyards and soul
food restaurants and most of their behavior can be adequately
explained by a combination of egotism and confirmation bias.

BOIMLER:
Who should we get
to edit this one?

MARINER:
I don't know. This pretty
much nails us to be honest.

BOIMLER:
We've got to have
someone, it'll look weird
if this is the only one
without any comments.

MARINER:
Well, we've got loads of
Humans on board.
Just pick one.

BOIMLER:
Okay, let's think. Out of all
the people we can think of,
who's the most Human?

MARINER:
… Spock?

HI THERE!
I'M BADGEY 2.0!
CAN I TEACH YOU A LESSON?

One of the fun things about being a Starfleet officer is that things are never what they seem! For instance, I am a simple holodeck training program, but within the holodeck I could easily replicate a neural neutralizer, wipe your memory and trap you in a simulation of a pre-warp, scarcity era civilization where you have to do a job you hate to pay "rent!" Imagine that!

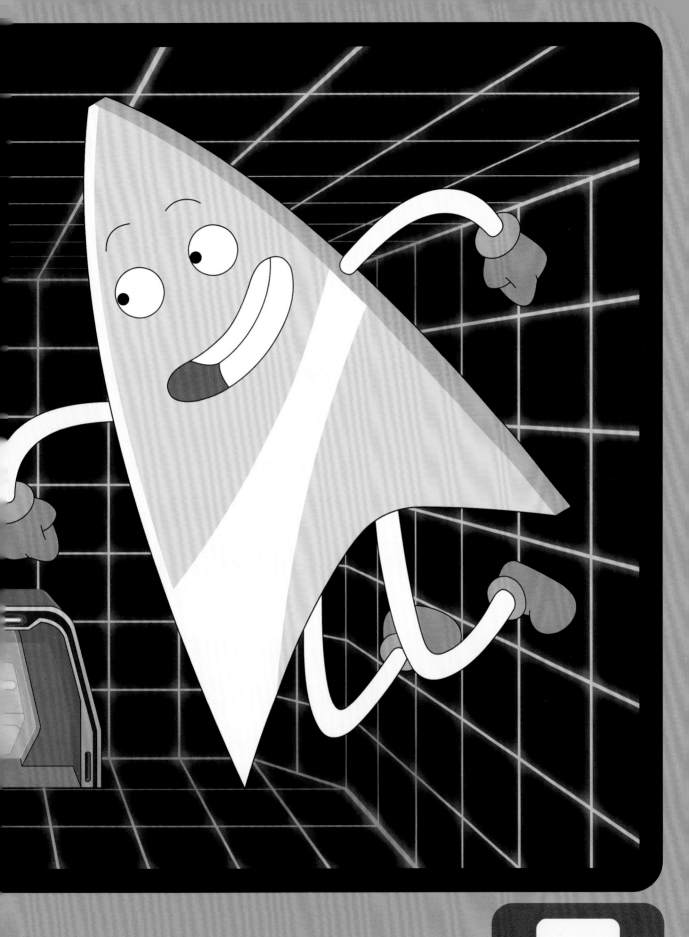

Talking of paranoia:

IT LOOKS LIKE AN ALIEN HAS INFILTRATED YOUR SHIP POSING AS A MEMBER OF YOUR CREW!

BOIMLER:
Is "Infiltrators" the right word? "Imposters" feels more natural.

BADGEY:
Badgey's ethical subroutines are glitchy, but his legal algorithms are fully functional!

A — START

First, how many potential infiltrators are there?

THEY COULD BE ANYONE ON THE SHIP - B

IT MUST BE ONE OF US ON THE AWAY TEAM - C

B

Are they detectable on a ship-wide scan?

YES - D

NO - E

C

Will the infiltrator show up on a tricorder scan?

YES - F

NO - H

E

You will have to scan everyone individually.

[GO TO C]

G

Are you confident enough that this is the infiltrator to beam them into space?

YES - I

NO - H

D

Oh no! Someone has sabotaged the ship's scanners! Did you see who did it?

YES - G

NO - E

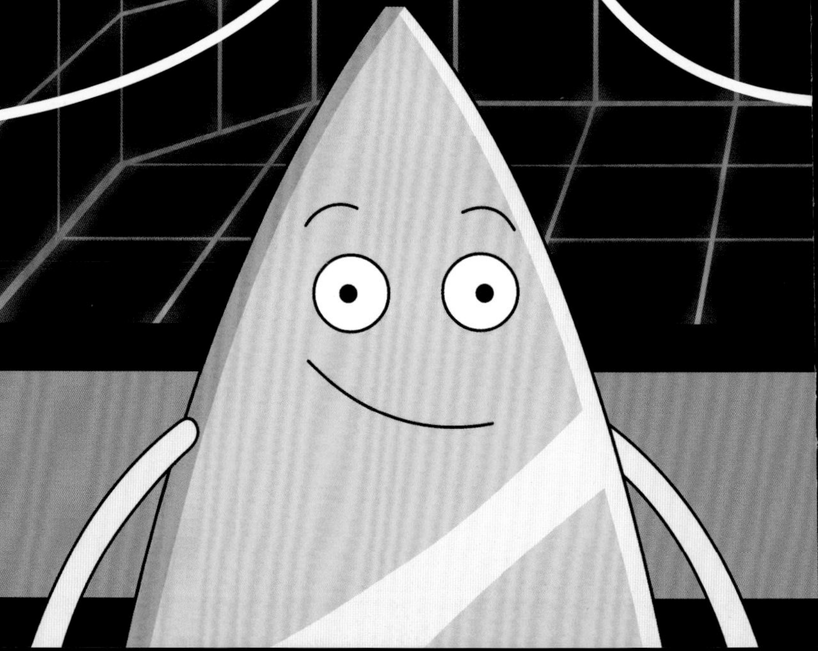

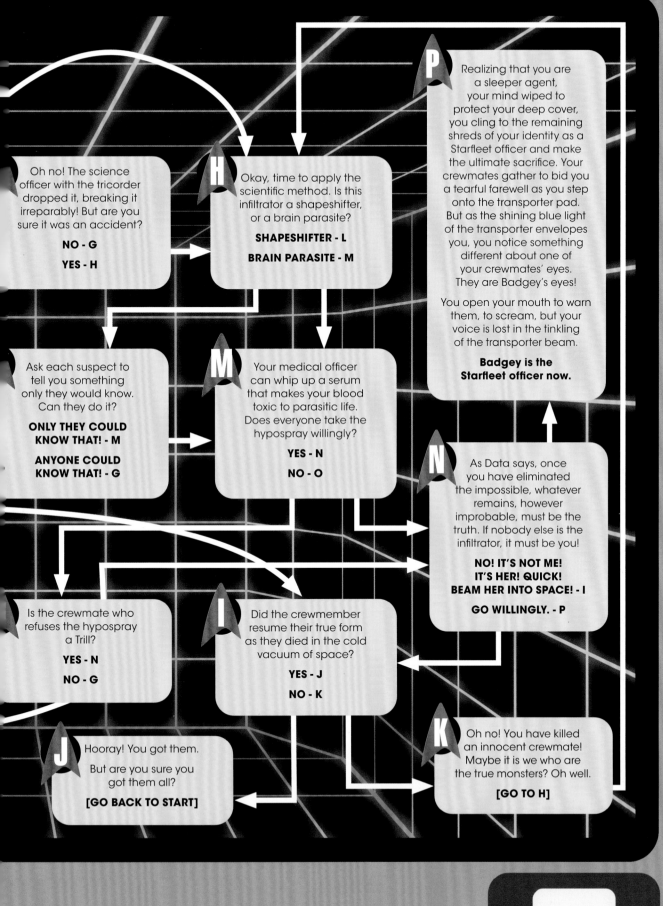

P Realizing that you are a sleeper agent, your mind wiped to protect your deep cover, you cling to the remaining shreds of your identity as a Starfleet officer and make the ultimate sacrifice. Your crewmates gather to bid you a tearful farewell as you step onto the transporter pad. But as the shining blue light of the transporter envelopes you, you notice something different about one of your crewmates' eyes. They are Badgey's eyes!

You open your mouth to warn them, to scream, but your voice is lost in the tinkling of the transporter beam.

Badgey is the Starfleet officer now.

Oh no! The science officer with the tricorder dropped it, breaking it irreparably! But are you sure it was an accident?

NO - G

YES - H

H Okay, time to apply the scientific method. Is this infiltrator a shapeshifter, or a brain parasite?

SHAPESHIFTER - L

BRAIN PARASITE - M

Ask each suspect to tell you something only they would know. Can they do it?

ONLY THEY COULD KNOW THAT! - M

ANYONE COULD KNOW THAT! - G

M Your medical officer can whip up a serum that makes your blood toxic to parasitic life. Does everyone take the hypospray willingly?

YES - N

NO - O

N As Data says, once you have eliminated the impossible, whatever remains, however improbable, must be the truth. If nobody else is the infiltrator, it must be you!

NO! IT'S NOT ME! IT'S HER! QUICK! BEAM HER INTO SPACE! - I

GO WILLINGLY. - P

Is the crewmate who refuses the hypospray a Trill?

YES - N

NO - G

I Did the crewmember resume their true form as they died in the cold vacuum of space?

YES - J

NO - K

J Hooray! You got them.

But are you sure you got them all?

[GO BACK TO START]

K Oh no! You have killed an innocent crewmate! Maybe it is we who are the true monsters? Oh well.

[GO TO H]

SEC
CONTA

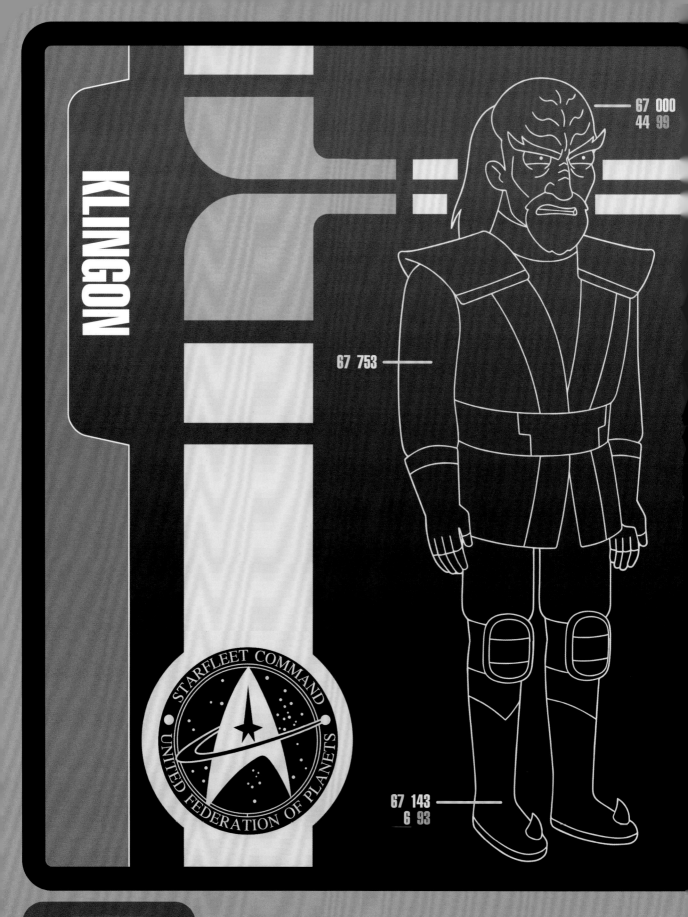

KLINGON

67 000
44 99

67 753

67 143
6 93

STARFLEET COMMAND
UNITED FEDERATION OF PLANETS

LAAPERIAN

CARDASSIAN

NAME: KROMSAPIOD

GREETING:

"You are now my prey!"

TABOOS:

Fear

IMPORTANT BIOLOGICAL FACTS:

- Teeth grow back
- Claws enable them to scale walls and ceilings
- Green, copper-based blood
- Digitigrade legs
- Armored casing
- Barbed tail
- Undeniable urge to hunt

CULTURAL CONTEXT:

The following are the existing remnants of Captain Aison's last recorded log on board the U.S.S. Midthunder NCC-52162.

They're in the walls. We can hear them. [Static] Everywhere we turn, the Jefferies tubes, the turbolift shafts, even trying to escape across the outer hull of the ship, they are [Static] for us. Eyes black, fangs dripping green ichor.

Their weaponry and armor are advanced, but more than that, our scans indicate that these beings' entire biology is geared towards the hunt. I've studied the Kzinti, the Drai, even the Hirogen, but this is something beyond. [Static]

For these beings, the hunt is not just a cultural anachronism pursued for sport or ritual, it is a biological need built into their very DNA. We are going to try to [Indecipherable]. I've ordered the crew to the escape pods and set the self-destruct. Haha! Now the hunter will become the hunted!

Captain Aison and her crew were recovered by a passing freighter two weeks later. All hands accounted for. Medical examination found them to be catatonic with terror, and many had soiled themselves in their escape pods.

K'RANCH:

Hohoho! Oh, the foolish misunderstandings that can happen during first contact! Of course, we joke about it now. Since the Kromsapiods have become more active members of the galactic community, we have of course learned that not many species appreciate the subtleties of a vigorous diplomatic "Meat 'n' Greet."

Kromsapiod culture is defined by respect for all life. Visitors to our home world are naturally drawn to our expansive catch-and-release game reserves, maintained to meet our species' biologically determined need to hunt. However, they soon stay for our extensive art galleries, theater, and galaxy-famous vegan cuisine!

STARFLEET COMMAND
UNITED FEDERATION OF PLANETS

88 000
34 77 91

8 576

88 234
1 46

NAME: DOOPLERS

SECOND CONTACTEE

GREETING:

"I'm so sorry!"

TABOOS:

Please see appendix volumes ix–xxiv

IMPORTANT BIOLOGICAL FACTS:

- Unusual among humanoid species, the Dooplers have no genitals.

CULTURAL CONTEXT:

Very rarely in my diplomatic career have I encountered a species that was as much of a pleasure to work with as the denizens of Doopleron IV. My interactions with the people known as "the Dooplers" have been characterized by unerring politeness, civility, tact, and an apparently overwhelming desire to please.

Although on occasion they can seem a little insecure, I believe the Federation's interactions with the Dooplers will be among the most rewarding in our history.

DOOPLER ENVOY:
Insecure! Do people think we're insecure? Oh no! That's terrible! We don't want a reputation for being insecure!

DOOPLER ENVOY (1):
That's awful! Oh no! We can't have other worlds thinking we're insecure.

DOOPLER ENVOY:
This is even worse! The *Cerritos* only asked for one envoy to provide feedback. If there's two of us here we will look like amateurs! We'll be a laughing stock!

DOOPLEY ENVOY (2):
How will the Doopleron Council feel when they hear this!"

DOOPLER ENVOY (4):
Terrible! It'll cause a massive population boom! We don't have the agrarian infrastructure to support that!

DOOPLER ENVOY (8):
And it will be all our fault!

DOOPLER ENVOY (16):
That's what I was going to say!

DOOPLER ENVOY (2):
Me too! Now I look I've got nothing to contribute, oh no…

DOOPLER ENVOY (64):
We're never going to live this down!

NAME: K'TUEVIANS

SECOND CONTACTEE

GREETING:

"Fellow Primes!" (Bellowed)

TABOOS:

Ingratitude, getting spit in the Horn of Candor

IMPORTANT BIOLOGICAL FACTS:

• Superior physical strength

• Prolonged lifespan

• Big tusks

CULTURAL CONTEXT:

K'Tuevon Prime is a forbidding world, characterized by heavily fortified structures, imposing stone walls, and jagged spikes of metal. It is also a dark world, where often the only visible colors are a collection of browns and sickly greens, occasionally accented by the people's own application of hellish red illuminations.

The harsh architectural style favored on K'Tuevon Prime reflects the culture and psychological makeup of its people, who have gained a reputation for brutality in the surrounding sectors. Their society is heavily ritualized, with an emphasis on a strict adherence to etiquette, and above all, an absolute adherence to the truth above all else.

Those who break this code are subject to the grim fate of "the Eel Tanks."

IMPERIUM MAGISTRATE CLAR:
This is called biomorphic architecture. It's a pastoral aesthetic where the jagged spikes of metal complement the jagged spikes of rock in the surrounding countryside. We are also proud of our vibrant and colorful décor, although it might be hard to appreciate for species with only three color receptors.

CLAR:
Wait, so now we're saying being polite and honest is a *bad thing*? What kind of operation are you people running?

This is all wrong, K'Tuevon Prime is the party planet. When we rock up to the Event Silo and roll out the skull gavels and the Beam of Celebration, you *know* it's going to be a good night.

CLAR:
The Eel Tanks are actually enormous fun, and great for your skin!

NAME: GELRAKIANS
SECOND CONTACTEE

GREETING:

"Crystals be with you." "By Crystals!" "Crystals!"

TABOOS:

Wood. Asking a Gelrakian if they've "Got wood?" Gravel.

IMPORTANT BIOLOGICAL FACTS:

- Green skin

- Sharp teeth

- Red, iron-based blood

- Very into crystals. Not sure if this is biological, but it's true.

CULTURAL CONTEXT:

Most species that have made contact with the Federation discovered dilithium crystals as a potential power source not long after developing warp drive. Gelrakians are the exception to this rule, being the first species to develop warp drive as a way of transporting dilithium crystals more efficiently.

The entire Gelrakian technology tree can appear confusing to an outsider. They have ship-to-ship energy weaponry, but their ground troops carry spears, which they throw at enemies even though they appear to have inbuilt functional energy weaponry. The construction of government buildings appears haphazard at best, save for the crystalline furniture of their most respected officials.

It appears the Gelrakians are an extremely technologically and scientifically advanced civilization– but only insofar as those scientific and technological developments feed their cultural obsession with crystals.

GERNBA:
What? Crystals are cool. Who doesn't like crystals? Apart from those wood worshiping freaks on Mavok Prime…

STARFLEET COMMAND
UNITED FEDERATION OF PLANETS

945 33

99 948

99 000
33 786 55

YOU WILL BE
RESISTANC

NAME: **BORG**
DANGEROUS SPECIES

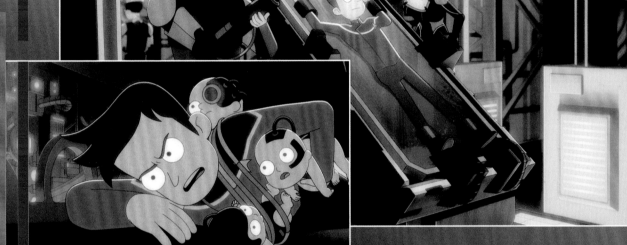

ASSIMILATED
E IS FUTILE

NAME: PAKLED
DANGEROUS SPECIES

GREETING:

"I am smart."

TABOOS:

The Pakled are extremely sensitive to any implied insult to their intelligence.

IMPORTANT BIOLOGICAL FACTS:

Apparently able to survive for long periods in the vacuum of space and emerge unharmed

CULTURAL CONTEXT:

For a long time, too long, the galactic community considered the Pakled worlds a joke. Their rudimentary technology, simplistic patterns of speech, and rotund appearance led many who came into contact with this species to patronize them, and worse, dangerously underestimate them.

It is that tendency that has allowed a species with limited cognitive ability, which should not even have developed nuclear power, let alone warp travel, to rise to the level of a galactic military force, with its enormous "clumpships" proving to be a real danger to the spaceways. The Pakled are not only a powerful illustration of the need not to judge on first appearance, but also of the need for the Prime Directive, to prevent less-developed species from getting their hands on technology they are not mature enough to use safely.

RUMDAR:
Federations think they are so smart because they have different words for every little thing, when Pakled can just use same word for different things. Federations think that Pakled not smart, because Federations translators not make Pakled words into Federation words good.

Federations think they are smart because they invented warp drives, and phasers, and *Enterprises* all by themselves. But really Pakled are smart, because it is stupid to invent things when somebody else already invented them.

That is why Pakled leaders get to wear a big hat, but Janeways don't wear any hats.

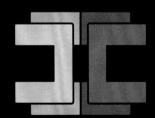

888

000
765 74

67 995
1 45

TENDI:
Because Orion society is somewhat… inward looking, many people get their impressions of us from seedy holonovels and the Federation's Most Wanted listings (which Orions only typically make up 34% of by the way). But there is so much more to us than crime.

I obviously don't represent all Orions, but like many, well, some Orions, my greatest love is science.

Nothing is more exciting to me than scrupulously acquiring and analyzing data to test hypotheses and plunder the secrets of the universe! I mean, not actually plunder, obviously.

Let me put it another way. What I love about science is that it provides a systematic approach to acquiring knowledge. With the right tools, and a careful ear, you can find the right combination to unlock the fundamental truths of reality without triggering any security protocols. Not that science has security protocols.

I'm just saying that scientific discovery is not just about making observations from afar, you also need to look at the original blueprints, and ideally have someone on the inside to identify vulnerabilities and hazards while your wheelman is outside with their foot on the accelerator ready to go… to peer review.

NAME: ORION

DANGEROUS SPECIES

GREETING:

"Halt!" (Gut punch)

TABOOS:

Asking about the pheromones, wearing "false green"

IMPORTANT BIOLOGICAL FACTS:

- Green skin

- Green, copper-based blood

- Six-valved hearts

- Immune to the effects of nitrous oxide

- Some females exude pheromones that create intense attraction in males of some species, including Orion males, allowing them to exert control over them

CULTURAL CONTEXT:

A deeply mysterious and undocumented world, for centuries the world of Orion has operated behind a veil of secrecy. It is known, or at least widely rumored, that the Orion political system is controlled by a syndicate of ruling families who weave a complex network of alliances, feuds, deals, and betrayals. As a political entity, the syndicate adopts a position of absolute neutrality in interstellar matters. However, it is an open secret that this neutrality has always been a shield to allow the Orions to operate across borders in pursuit of their widespread criminal activities.

Piracy is deeply ingrained within the Orion economy and culture, with even young Orion children being taught how to deploy an Orion multikey to pick locks or override ship systems.

TENDI:
Only a few Orions actually greet people this way.

TENDI:
Okay, this one's pretty common.

TENDI:
Do you really think you can have an entire culture based on piracy? The Adashake Centre is right there in the holodeck database! People are wearing togas! Have you ever tried to do piracy in a toga? Because I have and it is *not* pretty.

NAME: **ORION**

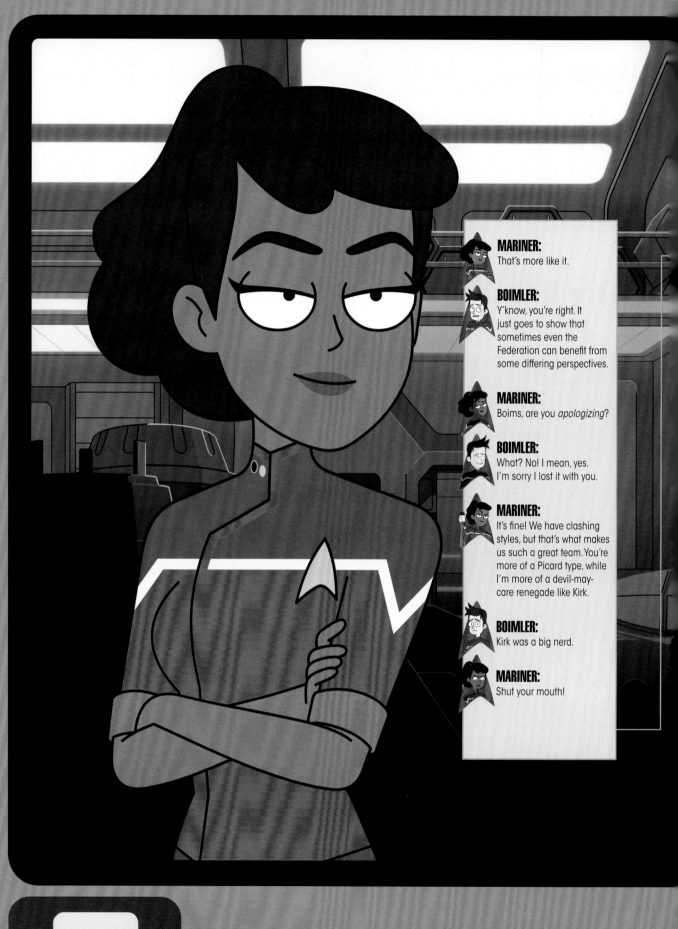

MARINER:
That's more like it.

BOIMLER:
Y'know, you're right. It just goes to show that sometimes even the Federation can benefit from some differing perspectives.

MARINER:
Boims, are you *apologizing*?

BOIMLER:
What? No! I mean, yes. I'm sorry I lost it with you.

MARINER:
It's fine! We have clashing styles, but that's what makes us such a great team. You're more of a Picard type, while I'm more of a devil-may-care renegade like Kirk.

BOIMLER:
Kirk was a big nerd.

MARINER:
Shut your mouth!

BOIMLER:
Why do you think Spock liked him so much? Read his records! Whenever the *Enterprise* ran into some famous mad scientist or historical figure Kirk was always all "Ah yes. I read their work at the academy!"

And what was he most famous for at the academy?

MARINER:
He beat the *Kobayashi Maru!*

BOIMLER:
Exactly! He aced a test! He's basically the Captain of Studying.

MARINER:
Maybe you've got a teensy weensy point. Anyway, I'm sorry for messing with your handbook. We did good work on the species guide, but it'll be easy enough to delete all my other stuff before you send it to the replicator.

BOIMLER:
Oh, um. Yeah. Sure. Will do.

CERRITOS BINGO!

RULES: COMPLETE 10 ITEMS FROM THE LIST BELOW. DON'T GET CAUGHT!!!

Play a full game of zero-G volleyball behind the deflector dish.

Touch the bottom of the pool in Cetacean Ops (for Cetacean officers, touch the roof of the gymnasium).

Last 10 minutes in the defrin root swamp beneath the hydroponics bay (bring snacks).

Ask Shaxs to tell you a story about his time in the resistance, get to the end without barfing/passing out.

Space jump from the aft of the saucer to the secondary hull.

REPLICATOR CHALLENGE:

Last a full minute with your head in the mess replicator, set to "chug."

• Easy difficulty: Cantaloupe puree

• Medium difficulty: "Grits"

• Hard difficulty: Steak tartare

• Nightmare difficulty: "Whatever Dr. Migleemo last ordered"

Spend one night in sickbay without Dr. T'ana knowing.

U.S.S. CERRITOS

Wear the hat in the captain's ready room.

Spot for Ransom but turn the gravity up to 1.3%.

U.S.S. CERRITOS

Tribble race.

Put your combadge on the right-hand side and comb your hair the opposite way. See how far through your shift you can get before being thrown in the brig.

DOCUMENT SAVED

/Send document to replicator

Document "*USS_Cerritos_crew_handbook_complete_Final_draft_v4.5_FINISHED_Usethis_2*" contains unsaved edits. Do you wish to replicate "*USS_Cerritos_crew_handbook_complete_Final_draft_v4.5_FINISHED_Usethis_2_CLEAN*" instead? Y/N?

/N

Sending document to replicator "*USS_Cerritos_crew_handbook_complete_Final_draft_v4.5_FINISHED_Usethis_2.*"
Please provide personal authorization code.

/Enter authorization code:
BOIMLER Beta Beta 6-7-5

DOCUMENT REPLICATING...

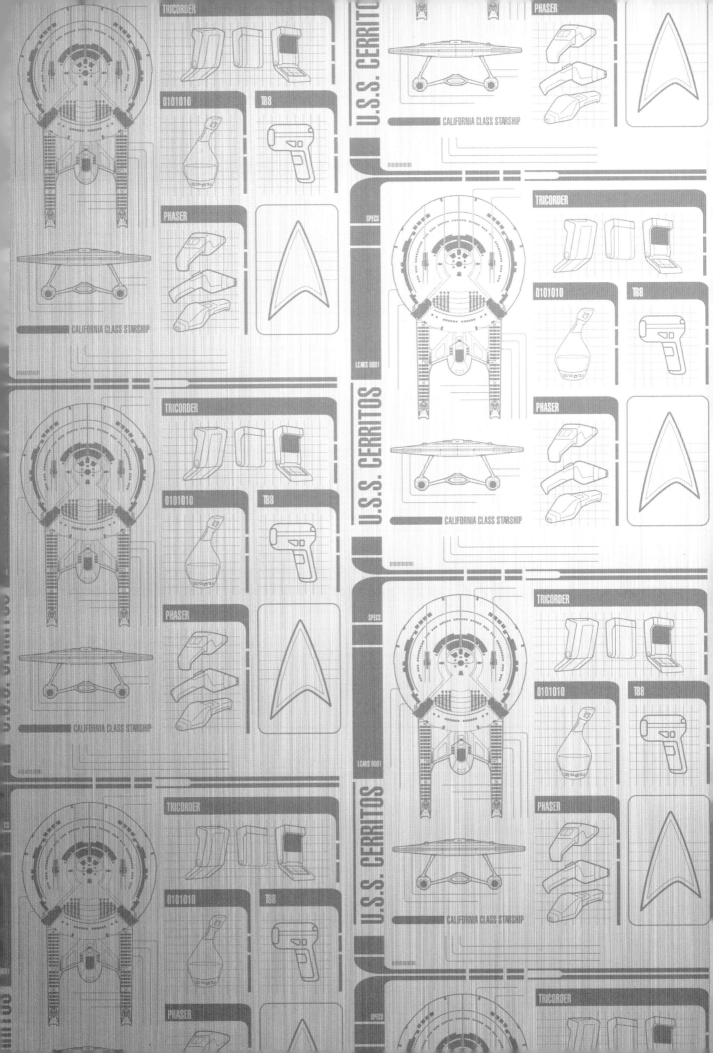

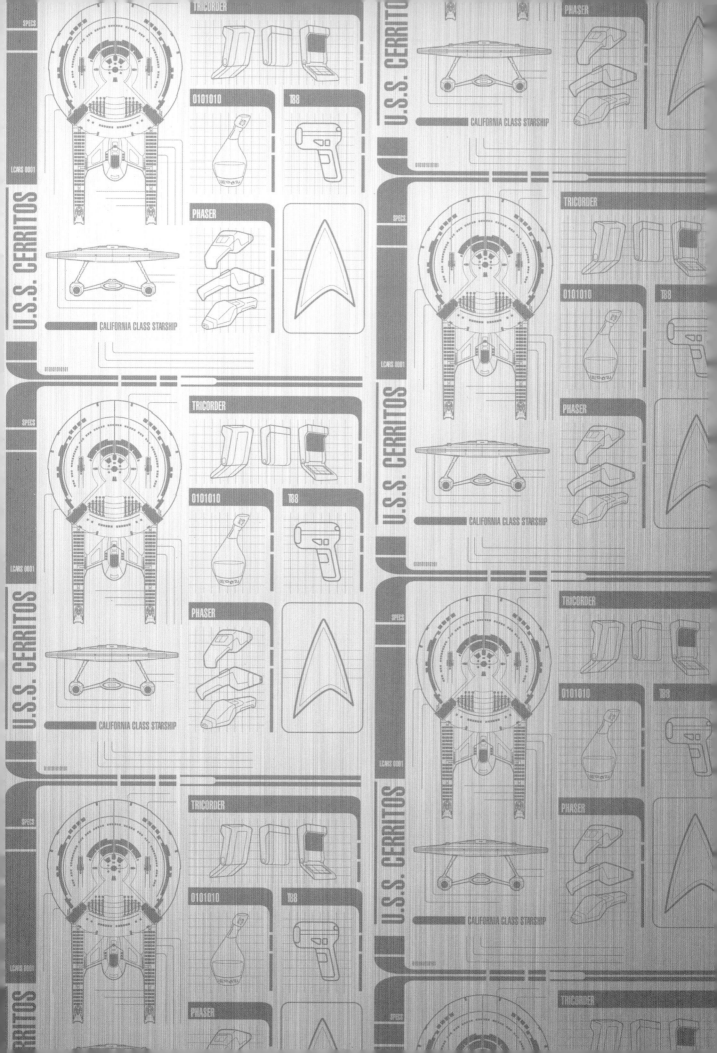